LUCI IN THE SPOTLIGHT

Church of Scotland

PRESENTED TO

Mairi Ogilvie
from
Balerno Parish
Church
Sunday Special.

Ballerinas
Luci in the Spotlight

Harriet Castor

*Hodder
Children's
Books*

a division of Hodder Headline plc

A Catalogue record for this book is available from the British Library

ISBN 0 340 65130 X

Typeset by Avon Dataset Ltd, Bidford-on-Avon, Warks

Printed and bound in Great Britain by
Cox & Wyman, Reading, Berks

Hodder Children's Books
a division of Hodder Headline plc
338 Euston Road
London NW1 3BH

For the first little M – who did a lot of typing

Part One

New Girls

One

As Sadie shoved her case – empty now that she'd finished her unpacking – under her bed, I glanced across at the pictures she'd stuck up on her bit of wall. Every one was of a ballet dancer, leaping through the air in a *grand jeté*, or balancing in an elegant *arabesque* and smiling as if it didn't hurt at all.

My side of our little bedroom looked rather different. I guess I must have been the only person in the whole school who didn't have a single picture of a dancer to put up. I had a map of Australia instead.

'Where's Sydney, then?' asked Sadie, kneeling next to me on my duvet and searching round the map.

'Down here – where the little flag's stuck in.'

'Oh, right.' She sat back on her heels so that she could look at the bottom of the picture. 'There's something written on it, really small—' Her nose was about three centimetres from the flag as she peered at it. ' "Dad"?'

'That's right. He gave me the map when I moved to England last spring with Mum, Frankie and my step-dad. The flag's so I won't forget where he is, he said.' I laughed. It seemed a bit dumb now I came to think of it.

'Wow!' Sadie frowned in thought for a moment. 'And it doesn't bother you?'

At the head of my bed was a little sash window. I pulled it up and leant out. 'What?'

'Not seeing your dad?' said Sadie behind me.

I shrugged. 'Can't be helped. I never got to see him much after the divorce anyway, even when we were living in the same city.' There was a big tree across the lawn. I checked out its lower branches – it looked like a great climber.

'Really?'

'Yeah. He and Mum would row horribly, even if they were just delivering or picking up Frankie and me from each other's apartments. So Mum sort of started forgetting to arrange visits.'

Away to the left, cars were crunching slowly over the gravel of the school driveway as the last few parents set off home again.

'Anyhow,' I said, 'living in England's cool – even if I do miss Dad.'

'You can say that again,' said Sadie. 'I'm getting goose pimples.' She shivered.

'Huh? Oh, sorry. I guess it is a bit draughty.' I shut the window and turned round. Sadie was back on her own bed. She picked up a framed photo

2

she'd put on her bedside locker.

'I couldn't bear not seeing my dad,' she said from behind it. Then I heard a sniff.

'Jeepers, Sadie!' I bounced across the room and made a flying snatch for the photo. Just as I thought. Sadie's eyes had gone watery and her chin was starting to wobble. 'Your folks only left a couple of hours ago!' I stuffed the photo under her pillow and put an arm round her shoulders. 'How are you going to last till half-term at this rate?'

'Sorry.' Sadie giggled apologetically and wiped her nose.

'Look,' I said, 'how about we go and see how Ella and Pippa are doing? They must have finished unpacking by now. I want to explore the school.'

'OK.' Sadie pushed herself off the bed and stood up.

Just at that moment we heard a knock on the door. Whoever it was didn't bother to wait for a reply – they just flung it open.

'More of my girls!' exclaimed a voice.

I turned to see a woman standing in the doorway, a delighted look on her face. She was wearing great billowing lengths of flowery material (probably supposed to be a dress, but you couldn't really tell).

Sadie sat back on the bed again, as if she'd been blown over.

'Dear hearts!' said the woman. 'I am Miss Lum, your matron. Now tell me – are you first years or second years?'

'First years, Miss Lum,' I said politely.

'Ah-ha!' Miss Lum's smile grew wider than ever. 'New to the school – just as I am. Thrilling!' She clasped her hands together, as if she was about to burst into song. But instead she said, 'And what are your names?'

'Sadie Marsh,' said Sadie.

'And I'm Luci Simpson,' I added. 'That's Luci with an "i".'

'How novel!' said Miss Lum enthusiastically. 'And you're Australian, if I'm not very much mistaken?'

I nodded.

'Charming!' Miss Lum beamed. 'It's wonderful to meet you, Sadie and Luci. I should warn you, though, that I'm sure to forget your names a moment from now. I have a brain like a sieve. Things just – ' and she wiggled her fingers, like falling rain ' – slip straight through. No matter! You shall find my room, dear hearts, on the landing. I am in charge of the whole of C corridor – that is, all the first and second year girls, I believe – and if you have any queries or . . . or *problems*, you must dash along to me straight away. Understood?'

Sadie and I nodded.

'Jolly good!' said Miss Lum, rubbing her hands together and retreating into the corridor. She half-turned to look at us again, and muttered to herself, 'How young, how talented they all look. Stars of the future – most certainly!' Then, with another ripple of her fingers, she sailed off along the corridor. 'See you later, dear hearts!'

Sadie and I looked at one another.

'Mad?' mouthed Sadie.

I nodded and grinned. 'As a hatter.'

Shutting the door of our room behind us, we made our way down the corridor in the opposite direction to Miss Lum. Four doors along, we came to a room marked:

C19
GABRIELLA BRUNI
PIPPA PARNELL-JAMES

I knocked.

'Come in!' called two voices together.

I turned the handle and tried to push the door back. It only budged a couple of centimetres, and then stuck.

'Hang on!' I heard Ella shout. There was a scuffling, and at last the door flew open.

'Sorry about that!'

Ella stood in the doorway, flushed and smiling. She'd scooped up several pairs of shoes in her arms and was trying to keep hold of them while she searched about for a clear bit of floor.

'Careful!' said Pippa, as a stray shoe escaped and bounced on the carpet. 'Those suede ones are ever so difficult to clean.'

'What on earth's going on here?' I asked.

5

'Unpacking of course!' Pippa turned towards me. Over each arm she had a pile of dresses, wrapped in those cellophane covers you get from the dry cleaner.

'You two have got so much stuff!' Sadie looked around at the mess in wonder. There were clothes covering the beds, the desk, the top of the chest of drawers and both lockers.

'Oh, none of it's mine,' said Ella. 'I've unpacked already.'

'You mean it all—'

'Belongs to me? Yes,' Pippa interrupted, flicking her blonde plait back over her shoulder. 'Well, we're here for weeks and weeks, aren't we? I thought the least they were going to do was give me a room to myself, with a proper large wardrobe. It's not as if I've brought *all* my clothes, anyway.'

'I have,' said Ella quietly.

I followed Ella's gaze to the wardrobe she and Pippa were having to share. You didn't need to be Sherlock Holmes to spot whose clothes were whose: Ella's were the two or three things not wrapped in cellophane, squashed forlornly at one end of the rail by the bulging mass of Pippa's dresses.

'I was going to suggest we go exploring,' I said. 'But I guess you're busy.'

'Exploring?' Pippa said, pulling out a drawer and trying to squash more into it, though it was full to bursting already. 'What for? Can't you remember your way round from the audition?'

The audition had been back in March. We'd had

6

to spend a whole weekend at the school. That's when the four of us had met.

''Course I can,' I said. 'But we only saw a few bits of the place then, didn't we? A studio, the dining hall and not much more. I want to check out every last corner of the building. It is our home now, after all!'

'Don't say that,' said Sadie quickly. All of a sudden her eyes were looking watery again.

'Aw, forget it!' I said cheerily. '*I'm* going exploring anyhow. I guess I'll just have to catch you guys later!'

I strode out of the room and started off towards the stairs. I wasn't surprised a second later to hear a rustle of cellophane, and then three pairs of feet hurrying after me.

'Hey, Luci!' called Sadie. 'Wait for us!'

Two

'Look! This is the studio we were in for the audition, remember, Pips?' I turned to Pippa, then looked back through the glass panel of the door.

'Don't call me—' began Pippa, but Sadie cut her off.

'Yes, and Ella and I were down the corridor in that one there!' she said, pointing to a wide swing door with a plaque saying 'Dempsey Studio' hanging above it. 'I was so nervous I thought I was going to be sick!'

'My teeth wouldn't stop chattering,' said Ella. 'Funny to think of it now, isn't it?'

'Now we're really here,' said Sadie, nodding. 'Now we're proper pupils of The Evanova School of Ballet.' She giggled. 'It feels weird just saying it!'

'When you think how many famous dancers have been here before us . . .' Ella gazed up at the rows of pictures that lined the walls of the corridor. 'Look at this one! It's Lily Dempsey.'

'Let's see!' We crowded round. I pushed myself up on the radiator to get a better look.

Lily Dempsey was probably The Evanova School's most famous former pupil. She'd danced with ballet companies all over the world.

'Hmm.' Pippa stared at the photograph critically.

'Her balance isn't quite right on that *attitude*.'

'I think she looks wonderful!' breathed Sadie. 'That tutu is gorgeous. And just look at the diamonds on her tiara!'

'They're not real, you know,' sniffed Pippa.

'I'd love to wear a costume like that,' said Ella dreamily.

'Oh, Ella! It'd look wonderful on you,' said Sadie. 'All that silver and white against your dark hair—'

'Rather you than me,' I muttered.

'Why?' Sadie looked at me. 'Wouldn't you love a costume like that too?'

I shrugged. 'Floaty skirts and lacy bits and frills? No fear! I don't think I've ever owned a party dress in my life.'

Three faces were gazing at me with a mixture of shock and pity. I laughed and looked back to the rows of pictures on the walls. 'This is more like it!' I said, pointing to a large photograph in a plain black frame.

It was Lily Dempsey again, but this time she didn't look anything like a fairy-tale princess. Her costume was a lycra bodysuit, with a bright pattern of multi-coloured stars all over it. Her pointe shoes were bright red and she was in the middle of a massive leap, with her arms above her head and her fingers splayed out like spiky spiders.

'You prefer that?' said Ella, staring at the photo and then at me really seriously, as if she was trying to work something out.

'No contest!' I said.

Then Sadie spotted the clock. 'Hey – hadn't we better be getting back?' she said. 'We're supposed to be in the dining hall at six-thirty.'

'But it's hardly even ten past,' I said, 'and we haven't been all the way down here yet.' I pointed ahead to where the corridor turned off to the right. 'Come on – there's bags of time.'

It was like one of those 'make your own adventure' books, where you find yourself in some castle full of rows and rows of doors. Every time you choose a door you turn to a different page to find out what's behind it. And it's either something magically wonderful, or it's a real disaster, and maybe you have to start the whole adventure again.

That's what I was thinking as we pressed on down the corridor, turning right, and then left and then right again. It seemed to snake on for ever, and it was getting creepier too, as the light outside faded and the shadows got thicker and blacker.

'Where are we now, then?' asked Ella at last, sounding a bit nervous.

I looked out of the nearest window. I could see a stretch of grass, and then some trees, but that didn't tell me much. The school grounds all looked the same to me.

'We're lost, aren't we?' said Pippa triumphantly. She turned to Ella. 'I told you she didn't know where she was going!'

'We are not lost!' I said quickly. 'I have a perfect sense of direction, thank you.'

I thought for a minute. The corridor stretched ahead of us into darkness, but I got the feeling it was taking us further away from the main bit of the school, not nearer to it. The simplest thing would have been to turn round and retrace our steps, but Pippa would have gloated if we'd done that. There was only one other option. To our right, there was a short passageway with a door at the end of it.

'It's down here,' I said.

'You sure?' Sadie came up to my shoulder.

'Absolutely.' I nodded. 'It should be a short-cut straight back to the dining-hall corridor.'

'OK then.'

We walked down the passage. The door at the end was in shadow.

'You first.' Sadie pushed me ahead of her.

'No – stop!' Ella, on my other side, grabbed my elbow. 'Look! It says' – she peered into the gloom – 'no entry.'

'Yes, and it'll be no entry because it's a really good short-cut,' I said, reaching out for the handle. 'You mark my words.'

I pulled the door open. Beyond it was another short corridor, with another door at the end of it. 'See?' I said over my shoulder, as the others followed behind.

Feeling more confident, I opened the second door and stepped through.

11

Three

I'd stepped into total darkness. But somehow, even without being able to see anything, I could sense it wasn't another corridor; it was a room.

'Where's the light switch?' whispered Sadie in my ear.

I fumbled for it on the wall. 'Can't – find – oh, there it is!'

I flicked the switch, and suddenly the room lit up before me.

'Wow!' Sadie stepped forward and turned around slowly, looking about her in wonder as if she'd just entered Aladdin's cave.

That wasn't such a bad description, actually. The lights I'd flicked on had red shades that made the whole room glow rosily. Heavy dark curtains were drawn across the window, and there was a richly patterned rug on the floor beneath our feet.

To our left was a marble fireplace, with a mirror hanging above it. To our right, the wall was completely covered in shelves, filled with row after row of old leather books.

'They're all about ballet!' exclaimed Sadie, peering at the titles on the spines. Ella hurried to her side to see.

'Where is *this* then?' said Pippa sharply. 'I thought

you said something about a short-cut, Luci?'

'Uh – straight ahead through there,' I said quickly, pointing to a door directly opposite the one we'd come through. It was ajar, but I could only see darkness beyond. 'This must be some sort of library for the teachers, I guess.'

Secretly I wasn't so sure, and I got an uncomfortable feeling I wanted to get out of there as soon as possible. But Sadie had already reached a book down from one of the shelves and was leafing through it with Ella.

'Wow! Look at these costume designs. This book must be really old!' I heard her say.

'It is,' came a sharp voice out of nowhere. 'And far too valuable to be pawed by inquisitive little girls. Put it back.'

Sadie gasped and the book slipped through her fingers. If Ella hadn't been right next to her to catch it, it would have hit the carpet the very next second.

I spun round to see where the voice had come from. Through the half-open door ahead, I could dimly make out two bony hands curled over the arms of a chair, and a vague shape of face and hair above them.

There was a click, and a whirring sound, and the shape floated towards us, into the light.

'Madame!' I heard Ella gasp and, like a ragged *corps de ballet*, we each bobbed down in a curtsey.

'Madame' is what everyone in the school calls Galina

13

Evanova, the headmistress. She used to be a ballerina, but she's ancient now – a little wrinkly old thing in an electric wheelchair, with a marshmallow cloud of white hair, and arms and legs so thin they look as snappable as breadsticks. Her eyes are beady, like a bird's, and her hands are like birds' claws too, with bony fingers and sharp-looking nails.

I'd seen her once before – she'd watched part of Sadie's audition back in March – but I'd never heard her speak. Her voice was surprisingly crisp and strong.

'What are you doing here?' she said now, looking at each of us in turn with a fierce expression.

'It – it's my fault, Madame,' I began. 'We were exploring and . . . well, I thought this was a short-cut.'

Madame gave me a very direct stare, as if she was trying to see right through me to the wall behind. 'A short-cut? To where?'

'The dining hall, Madame,' I said.

'The dining hall?' Suddenly Madame threw her head back and laughed. I could see a flash of gold somewhere in amongst her back teeth.

Then she looked at us again, with no hint of a smile. 'This,' she said, 'is my apartment. My *private* apartment.' She rolled the 'r' on the word 'private' for emphasis. 'Never – but *never* – does anyone come in here unless I summon them.'

'Yes, Madame,' we all murmured.

'Curiosity killed the cat, child,' she said to me. 'You

14

would do well to remember that. Now go – all of you.'

We hurried to the door. I saw that Sadie – who's pale at the best of times – had gone almost blue with fright, and even Ella's olive complexion seemed to have lost its colour.

'One last thing,' said the voice behind us. Clustered at the door, we turned back to face Madame.

'What are your names?' she said.

I stepped forward. 'I'm Luci Simpson, Madame,' I said. 'And these are—'

'Do they not have voices of their own?'

I clamped my mouth shut.

'Sadie Marsh, Madame,' said Sadie in a tiny voice.

'Gabriella Bruni, Madame,' said Ella.

'Pippa Parnell-James, Madame.'

Madame looked twice at Pippa. 'Ah,' she said, raising an arched eyebrow, and extending one talon-like finger in Pippa's direction. 'Clara Parnell's child?'

'Yes, Madame,' said Pippa proudly. Clara Parnell – her mum – used to be a really famous ballerina, as Pippa's always reminding us.

Madame nodded, and looked around the four of us again. 'I shall be watching you all,' she said, and since I could very well imagine her as some ghost-like presence staring out of every shadow, this thought sent a shiver up my spine. 'I never forget a face or a name. Never. Now – you may go.'

We tumbled out into the corridor and shut the door behind us. For a moment we simply stood there, breathing hard, and then I felt a strange giggly feeling welling up in me, like you sometimes get after a ghost train ride or a scary film.

'I never forget a face or a name!' I said, putting on Madame's voice.

'Shh! She'll hear you!' Sadie flapped her hands at me anxiously.

When we were safely through the next door and back in the main corridor, Ella whispered, 'You know that means she'll think badly of us forever – right till we leave the school!'

Sadie looked genuinely frightened. 'Do you think so?'

'Ah – don't be silly,' I said. 'We got lost, that's all. It wasn't our fault, she knows that.'

'Yes,' said Pippa, looking down her nose at me. 'It wasn't *our* fault, Luci Simpson. It was yours.'

I looked at her crossly and opened my mouth to speak. But then I shut it again and swallowed hard. 'All right,' I said at last. 'I'm sorry, guys. I guess I did lead you the wrong way.'

'We've still got to get to the dining hall,' said Sadie, looking round for a clock. 'And – oh, blimey! – we're late for supper now. Which way is it?'

Before I could say anything, Ella pointed to the left. 'I think we should go back the way we came. *This* way.'

'But look,' I said, 'since we've come this far, can't we just see what's along there?' I pointed to the right. 'There's that little door at the far end and I reckon—'

16

'*No!*' said Pippa, Sadie and Ella together.

'OK, OK,' I laughed, as they grabbed my arms and steered me back along the corridor. 'I was only joking.'

Four

We *were* late for supper, and there was nothing but corned beef and mashed potato left, which earnt me a few fiery looks from Pippa. I ignored them. I was more worried about us getting into trouble with the teacher on duty, but luckily no one seemed to notice as we came into the dining hall, and slid into some spare seats at the nearest of the long tables.

The noise of hundreds of voices, chattering excitedly, rose above the scrape and clatter of knives and forks on plates.

'Who's taking us for *pas de deux* this term?' I heard, further down our table.

'Who cares? As long as I don't have to dance with Darren again.'

'At least he can lift you, Stacey! I saw Nigel Watkinson a minute ago, and he doesn't look any better than last term. He's still got arms like pieces of string . . .'

Beside me, Sadie and Ella seemed too stunned by our encounter with Madame to feel like chatting. Opposite, Pippa was prodding a lump of corned beef, her nose wrinkled in disgust.

'If you don't want that, I'll have it,' I said to her when I'd wolfed down mine.

Pippa pushed her plate across the table towards

18

me. 'I don't know how you can eat that rubbish,' she said. 'It's horrid – and so fattening.'

I shrugged, and scraped her dinner on to my plate.

'Do you calorie count too?' asked a voice enthusiastically. It was a girl a couple of seats along from Pippa. The way she said it, you'd have thought it was a hobby – like train spotting or stamp collecting.

Pippa nodded. 'Mummy's always taught me to be careful about what I eat.'

The girl pushed her tray along the table and moved up into the seat next to Pippa's. 'So has my mother!' she said. 'I'm Shona Farley, by the way. I'm a new first year. You too?' She looked round at the four of us.

We nodded.

Sadie put down her fork. 'Hang on – I recognise you from the audition,' she said. 'You were in the same group as Ella and me, weren't you?'

Shona studied Sadie for a moment with a slight frown, then her face broke into a smile. 'That's it! I remember now. You're the one Madame told off about keeping your knees straight, right?'

Sadie blushed. 'Right,' she mumbled and hurriedly went back to her dinner.

'Well, how nice!' said Shona, still beaming. She turned to Pippa again. 'I can't believe the food they serve here though, can you? It *is* a ballet school after all – you'd think they'd be helping us slim. I mean, there's pudding with custard and everything!'

'I know,' said Pippa with a sigh.

19

'Why do they do it?' Shona shook her head in wonder.

'Because it tastes nice?' I offered brightly, shovelling another forkful of mashed potato into my mouth.

Shona and Pippa looked at me as if I was mad. Shona leant forward seriously. 'Have you never thought about dieting?' she asked.

'Nope,' I said. 'Never.'

Shona glanced at Pippa, who had a 'I might have known' expression on her face.

'You mean you don't even count how many calories you eat a day?'

'Nope,' I said again.

Shona looked as if she couldn't quite take that idea in. 'How much do you weigh?' she asked, looking up and down the bit of me she could see above the table.

'No idea,' I said.

At this, Shona looked like she was going to fall off her chair. She shook her head again, and bit into the apple she was holding. 'Some people!' she said.

After a few seconds of chewing, she turned back to Pippa. 'I've made a chart showing what I eat every day and my weight. I've got it stuck up on the inside of my locker door. There's a square to fill in each night. Do you want to come and see it some time? I could draw one up for you, if you like.'

For once, Pippa looked really interested. 'Great!'

'I've got some bathroom scales, too,' Shona added.

'I thought scales were banned?' said Ella, looking

puzzled. 'At my medical, Dr Payne told me she's the only one allowed to weigh us, to make sure we don't worry about it.'

Shona leant forward across the table with a laugh. 'Dr Payne's the one who's the worry-bug,' she said. 'It's a silly rule! I smuggled the scales in at the bottom of my suitcase and now I've got them under my bed.'

'Can I borrow them?' Pippa asked eagerly.

'Of course,' said Shona. 'Only don't let Miss Lum see you, OK?'

I turned to Sadie to see if she thought Pippa and Shona were completely crazy, like I did. But Sadie wasn't paying attention. She was staring at her plate of food, and biting her lip in worry.

Later that evening, when we were back in our room getting ready for bed, I noticed Sadie looking down at herself anxiously, pinching the skin on her tummy.

'What's the matter?'

She frowned. 'Do you think I ought to calorie count like Pippa and Shona?'

'No! Calorie counting is the stupidest, most boring thing in the world.' I threw back the bedclothes and climbed in. 'Anyway, going on a diet while you're still growing is dangerous. My dad said so and he's a doctor, so he should know.'

'Oh.' Sadie seemed to feel better at that.

'Take no notice of the others,' I said, bashing on my pillow to fluff it up a bit. 'It's a craze, that's all.

They'll get over it.' I turned off my bedside light and shut my eyes.

'Luci?' came Sadie's voice through the dark.

'Hmm?'

'You . . . you've got all your own opinions. I mean – you don't do things just because someone else says so. I think that's great.'

'Uh – thanks,' I said uncertainly. I wasn't quite sure what Sadie was on about, but I felt too dozy to ask. 'Sleep well.'

'You too.'

Five

That night I dreamt I was lost in unending shadowy corridors, and every time I opened a door, I found Madame behind it. When she grinned all her teeth were gold. I woke up with the fixed idea that she'd crept into our room in the night and was hiding in the wardrobe, and Sadie laughed at me because I insisted on opening the door to check.

I forgot about her, after that. But later in the day, I had a sudden horrible thought. We'd just been fitted with our new pink satin shoes, ready for our first ballet lesson the next morning. Now we were supposed to be sewing the ribbons on.

'Hey!' I said suddenly, putting down my cotton reel. 'Madame's not going to be taking our ballet lessons, is she?' I wasn't sure I was quite ready to meet those beady eyes again.

Pippa shook her head and squinted at the needle she was trying to thread. 'Madame only teaches the fifth formers, and only – bother! missed again! – only the very best ones even then. Mummy says it's a real honour to be picked for her class.'

'Some honour!' said Ella. 'I'd be hopeless. I don't think I could do a single *plié* in front of her after yesterday. She scares me stiff!'

'Who *will* be teaching us then?' asked Sadie. She

23

was clutching her shoes and stroking them as if they were little guinea pigs.

'Miss Latimer,' said a voice behind us.

'Youch!' My needle jabbed into my thumb.

'Oh, sorry – did I startle you?' Shona looked in from the corridor. 'I was just passing and I . . .' She held up her own ballet shoes. 'Mind if I borrow your sewing stuff?' Without waiting for an answer she came in and sat down, not noticing the looks Pippa, Sadie, Ella and I were exchanging. Was she going to hang around us like this all term?

'I heard some of the second years talking about Miss Latimer last night,' Shona went on, reaching for the pink thread.

'Did they say what she's like?' asked Sadie.

'All right, apparently. She was a good dancer in her day. Famous for all those roles in long white floaty dresses.'

'Ugh!' I stuck my tongue out and the others laughed.

'Pretty strict, though. And she's a shocker for having favourites, they said.'

'Favourites?' I asked.

Shona nodded. 'It seems you always know what she thinks of you by where she makes you stand in the room. All her top people go in the front row, the people she's not so keen on go in the middle row, and the real dorks are in the back row.'

'But that's horrid!' said Sadie.

'Look on the bright side,' I said. 'At least you

know where you stand with her.'

Sadie looked at me blankly.

'Get it?' I nudged her. 'Know where you stand? Oh, never mind! Can someone pass me the scissors?'

Six

It didn't take long for me to work out where *I* stood with Miss Latimer. First thing the next morning, I was at the barre in Dempsey Studio, with my feet sandwiched – toe-to-heel and heel-to-toe – in my very best fifth position. I was just beginning to wonder whether I'd tied the ribbons on my shoes too tightly, when – exactly as the long hand of the studio clock ticked on to eight forty-five – Miss Latimer walked in.

Or rather, wafted in, I should say. She didn't bob up and down like most people do when they walk – she sort of skimmed along, as if she was on one of those airport moving walkways.

When she got to the centre of the studio she stopped, and rested one hand on her chest. 'Girls,' she said, with a flutter of her eyelashes, 'I am Miss Latimer, your ballet mistress. And this' – she waved vaguely behind her – 'is your pianist, Mr Judd.'

Mr Judd, who'd followed Miss Latimer into the room, looked sort of saggy, like an old balloon that's half gone down. He was very tall, but so round-shouldered he reminded me of a tortoise, carrying his shell on his back.

Miss Latimer, on the other hand, was tiny and pale, like a porcelain doll. She had a long chiffon scarf round her neck and her eye shadow was bright mauve.

'Let me look at you all.' Miss Latimer stalked along the room, studying us carefully, and occasionally saying, 'hmm', or clicking her tongue in a dissatisfied way. Mr Judd, sitting at the piano, followed her with his eyes like a sad dog. I decided Mr Judd must be in love with Miss Latimer and that she despised him. That was why he looked so forlorn.

'Now, girls, *pliés*.'

Miss Latimer turned to Mr Judd and tapped out the speed of music she wanted. 'Four-four time. Andante, if you please.'

I tried my best in every single exercise, pointing my feet as hard as I could, and throwing myself into each movement with all my energy. In my first lesson as an Evanova pupil, I wanted to make a good impression.

But when, after the barre, Miss Latimer summoned us into the centre of the studio, Sadie, Ella and Pippa were put in the front row, while I ended up at the back.

I soon realised that Miss Latimer ignored most of the people on my row, as if they weren't there at all.

But I wasn't so lucky.

'You – carrot-top!' she said, when we'd just finished a *glissade* exercise. It took me a moment to work out who she was talking to, as my hair is *not* carrot-coloured – it's a sort of russet brown.

'Yes, Miss Latimer?'

'What is your name?'

I told her.

'And have you had ballet lessons before?'

I felt myself blushing. 'Loads!'

'Who was your teacher?'

'Jill Moreton, at the Moreton Academy in Sydney. Australia,' I added, just in case she hadn't cottoned on.

Miss Latimer gave a tinkling little laugh. 'Ah, no wonder you dance like a kangaroo!' she said. And she returned to the front of the studio to demonstrate the next exercise.

'Luci!' Two exercises later, Miss Latimer clapped her hands together to signal that the music should stop.

Over the piano lid, Mr Judd's face appeared to see what was up.

'You are dancing like a boy!' said Miss Latimer with a shudder. 'You should be the swan princess, not the warrior prince!'

She skimmed over the floor in my direction, and placed herself behind me. The girls in the rows in front parted so that we could see ourselves in the mirror.

Miss Latimer took hold of my wrists and moved my arms gently, wafting them in front of my body each in turn.

'See?' she said. In the mirror I saw she had a dreamy look in her eyes. 'That's the feeling we want. Think of feathers drifting on the breeze, of misty mornings in summer meadows.'

I had to try really hard to keep a *yuck* look off my face. This reminded me of the very first ballet teacher I'd had back home when I was three or four. She'd spent her whole time getting us to play 'let's pretend'. For the girls that meant flitting about being leaves, or butterflies, or fairies. It was the boys who got to be the good things, like horses and clowns and storm clouds shooting down their lightning.

Miss Latimer stood back and told me to do the step again on my own.

Desperately I tried to look wafty. It felt stupid.

'Ye-es,' said Miss Latimer uncertainly. 'You're *beginning* to get it.'

She walked back to the front of the class.

'Pippa – show Luci the *temps levé*.'

I knew by this time that Miss Latimer thought Pippa was the best thing since sliced bread. She couldn't even look at her without the edges of her mouth curling upwards like those fortune-telling fish you get in Christmas crackers.

Pippa simpered in a self-satisfied way and demonstrated the step. I stood there with one hand on my hip. *Temps levé* is just the posh ballet term for a hop, so it wasn't exactly that difficult.

'Superb!' Miss Latimer purred, pouting her lips as if she was trying to pronounce a French word. Then she turned to me. 'You see, Luci? That's the lightness I'm looking for. It must be graceful,

29

effortless, not like a warm-up for the Olympic high jump.'

The rest of the class laughed at this, and I laughed along too. But inside, I was scowling.

At the end of class we piled out of the studio, steaming like work-horses from the effort of trying to get our *changements* and our *échappés sautés* just how Miss Latimer wanted them.

It was a race down to the basement changing room, to see who could bag some room on the bench first. Miss Latimer might have wished I was more delicate in class, but when it came to elbowing my way through crowds afterwards, I won hands down every time.

'Here – I've saved you a space,' I said when Sadie, with lots of 'excuse me's' and 'sorry's' had finally managed to apologise her way through the crush.

'Thanks.' Sadie flopped down beside me and began pulling at the ribbons tied round her ankles.

'Isn't Miss Latimer wonderful?' breathed Shona, as she squeezed past. 'She's so thin!'

'I don't like her,' I said, slinging my ballet shoes into my rucksack crossly.

'She did pick on you rather a lot,' said Sadie.

'It didn't seem fair,' added Ella, taking the pins from her bun and shaking out her dark pony-tail. 'It wasn't as if you were getting the steps wrong.'

Pippa was by the mirror, standing sideways to admire her waist. Now she turned to face me. 'It's all a question of style,' she declared loftily. 'It's the *way* you do the steps she doesn't like.'

'I can't help it, can I?' I retorted. 'I mean – it's fine if you're good at wafting around like a fairy. Like you three—'

'Us? Fairies?' said Sadie.

'You know what I mean. All that dreamy stuff. I can manage it for about two steps, but then I lose it again. I hate dancing that way. It's just not me.'

'And you hate frilly costumes too!' laughed Ella, pulling on her blue school skirt. 'What *do* you like about ballet, Luci?'

I thought it over for a moment. 'I love the exciting steps. Big leaps. Spins. Those jumps where you cross your legs over lots of times in the air—'

'*Batterie*, they're called,' said Pippa. 'And they're boys' steps, mostly.'

'They are not!' I said quickly. 'Girls have to dance like that in loads of ballets these days.'

'And you're brilliant at jumps!' said Sadie, as she peeled off her pink tights. 'I watched you when we split up into groups for those *assemblés*. You jump the highest in the whole class!'

'I bet you'll be the best of all of us when we start jazz dance lessons in the second year,' said Ella. 'I tried jazz at my last school and I was hopeless!'

'Well, it's not much use to me now, is it? Miss Latimer just thinks I'm a kangaroo!' I said.

Pippa giggled, but when she saw the look I shot her, she cleared her throat and busily started rummaging in her school bag for something.

'I like the way you dance,' said Ella decidedly. 'You

31

know how teachers are – they get to think their way of doing things is the *only* way. I wouldn't worry about Miss Latimer if I were you.'

I was kneeling on the floor now, scrabbling under the bench for my school shoes.

'No fear!' I said when I emerged. 'Can you see me turning all airy-fairy just to please her?'

And at that thought, my three friends laughed almost as loudly as me.

Part Two
Odd One Out

Seven

'Hmm.' Miss Stretton, the deputy headmistress, sighed as her eyes flicked down the page of the black mark book.

'Running in the corridor three times this week,' she said. 'And' – her eyes narrowed – '*shouting* in the library?' She looked up at me sharply.

I shifted from foot to foot. It had been Guy Jenkins' fault. He was the loudest boy in our class, the sort who thought it was funny to sing the *Neighbours* theme tune every time I walked past. This time he'd asked me why I didn't have corks dangling from the brim of my school hat, too.

So I'd let out a kung-fu whoop and given him a super-ballistic Simpson wrist twist (though luckily Mr Bretherton, the librarian, hadn't seen that bit).

It had certainly shut Guy up for a while. But I had a hunch it'd be no use explaining *that* to Miss Stretton.

'Sorry, Miss Stretton,' I muttered, digging my toe into the blue splodge on her patterned carpet.

Miss Stretton made her fingers into a steeple and looked at me over them coldly.

'*Are* you sorry, Luci? Are you *really*?'

Changing feet, I dug at the red splodge instead.

'Stand still when I'm talking to you, child!'

I snapped to attention like a soldier.

'It seems to me, Luci,' said Miss Stretton, jutting her head forwards accusingly, 'that you have a problem. I suspected it from the very first moment I saw you at the audition last March. You think' – and she let out a little snort, as if it was a ridiculous idea – 'you think that you know best.'

She sounds just like Miss Latimer, I thought to myself.

'. . . nothing but unladylike, undisciplined behaviour. It may be acceptable these days in . . . in Sydney, or wherever it is you come from – but it is not acceptable here.' Miss Stretton jabbed her finger on the desk top, like she was trying to squash a beetle.

'You have been with us precisely five weeks now, Luci. I am aware that some pupils need time to settle down. But you have had long enough. I am beginning to feel that you do not fit in at this school.'

I sighed. Half-term was less than a week away, and I couldn't wait to get home for a few days. I fitted in *there*, at least.

As Miss Stretton rambled on, I pictured Mum in her place, with her crazy earrings and wild hair – just as frizzy as mine – which she piled on top of her head and tied with a scraggy scarf or (if she wasn't going out) fixed in place with a couple of knitting needles. I wondered what Miss Stretton would think of *her*.

'Is there something you find funny?' Miss Stretton snapped.

I realised I was grinning. Quickly I straightened my face. 'No, Miss Stretton.'

'I should think not.' She sucked in her breath. I half expected it to come out again as smoke. 'I cannot see that *you*, of all people, have anything to smile about.'

Sadie was waiting for me in the cloakroom when I got out. 'How was it?'

I picked at the edge of someone's boater. 'Usual stuff,' I said, flicking the bit of straw away. Then I pressed my fingertips together and fixed Sadie with a Miss Stretton look. 'No fun to be had at any time, child. On pain of death!'

Sadie giggled. 'I can just imagine her saying that, too!'

'I'd better not get into any more trouble before half-term, though,' I said. 'I think she'd boil me in oil if she found me outside her door again.'

'Oi! You two!' The cross face of a prefect appeared above the next row of blazers. 'Aren't you supposed to be in the playground? Scram!'

35

'Well, only four more days to go,' said Sadie as we stomped outside. 'I think even you can manage that.'

Eight

If Sadie thought I could manage four trouble-free days, she'd bargained without Miss Latimer. She seemed more and more annoyed with me each time I saw her – and now I couldn't get through a single ballet lesson without being told off for something.

The next morning's class was a case in point. By twenty past nine, Miss Latimer had already shouted at me for *tendu*ing too sharply, for not *frappé*ing sharply enough and had told me my *grands battements* were like a can-can routine. Now we were starting on *pirouettes* and I wondered what she was going to find wrong with them.

'*Temps levé, chassé, pas de bourrée*,' chanted Miss Latimer, as she demonstrated the steps, 'and *pirouette*. Finishing in a nice neat fifth position, of course, girls.'

Watching her, I wished I was one of those people who could sail round in a *pirouette* like they've got all the time in the world and they're never going to overbalance. But I'm not. I have to fling myself round as quickly as possible to stand a chance of facing the front again in one piece.

'Let's try it once all together,' instructed Miss Latimer, 'then we'll split up into groups. Ready – *and*!'

This was the cue for Mr Judd to start playing. As

37

the piano plinked and plonked its tune, I *temps levé*'d, *chassé*'d and *pas de bourrée*'d as best I knew how. And everything would have worked out fine, if the ribbons on one of my ballet shoes hadn't at that very moment decided to unravel themselves. So when I prepared my feet in fourth position, I didn't realise that I was standing on them. And when I snatched one foot under me and aimed the other up towards my knee, where it was supposed to stay glued as I twizzled round, I heard a ripping sound as the ribbon tore off the shoe, and my leg jerked off-balance.

By this time I'd flung my right arm out to launch me round, so I careered off in a half-slide, half-fall, and cannoned straight into Mary-Beth Lacey, who was timidly attempting her own *pirouette* next to me.

'Yiiiiikes!' I heard myself shout, as the studio dipped and spun and the floor suddenly swung up to try and hit me in the face. The next thing I knew, I'd landed in an untidy heap, with Mary-Beth somewhere underneath me.

For a moment there was a stunned silence. Mr Judd's hands hovered above the piano keys.

Hurriedly, I scrambled up. 'Sorry, Mary-Beth!'

I grabbed her elbow and tried to pull her to her feet, hoping she'd smile and say she was fine, and we could forget the whole thing.

But Mary-Beth wouldn't be pulled. She stayed where she was, sitting on her bottom, with her legs stuck straight out in front of her, toes pointing to the ceiling, like a doll. And one millisecond later, she burst into a fit of horribly loud, squelchy tears.

'Waaa!'

Blast it, I thought. If I was going to mow someone down, why did I have to choose the biggest cry-baby in the class?

'Luci Simpson!' Miss Latimer bawled over the noise. 'I've had just about enough of you!'

'But it wasn't my fault! I never—'

'You are a disruption in my class! Out!' she screeched, flinging a finger towards the door and looking as if she was about to explode. 'Get out! *Now*!'

There was no point in arguing. I ran.

Nine

As the studio door banged shut behind me, I stood
stock-still for a moment, my heart thudding so hard
in my chest I thought it would burst. Then I looked
down. Two pink ribbons were dangling from my right
shoe like ironed snakes. One of them was only
hanging on by a single tuft of thread.

Dratted things! I kicked my leg and the shoe flew
off and skidded on the shiny floor, spinning to a stop
halfway down the corridor. If only they'd let me keep
my old leather ballet shoes with the elastic, none of
this would have happened.

I stomped up and down the corridor several times.
Away at the far end, in Tyrrel Studio, the boys in our
year were in the middle of their class with Mr
Edwards, their ballet master. It sounded like he was
working them hard.

'Guy Jenkins! Can't you jump higher than that,
boy?'

As I strode past Dempsey Studio again, I heard
Mr Judd start up with some rousing chords, and swing
into a wonderfully energetic piece of music. Cross
as I was, I just couldn't help moving to it. And with
no Miss Latimer to tell me off, I could dance exactly
the way I wanted . . .

I leapt and bounded along the corridor, twisting,

spinning, stretching my arms in whatever direction and shape the music seemed to be telling me. I imagined myself doing a solo on stage. This was what real dancing felt like! I made up new steps, I *jeté*'d and twirled in combinations I'd never tried before.

And, as the music built to its ending, I prepared my feet in fourth position, whipped round in a perfect *pirouette* and landed kneeling on one knee, with my arms up in fifth above my head.

I could see my reflection in the glass of the fire door not far in front of me. One day, I thought, looking at my arms curving above my head – one day, this will be a picture on the corridor wall, up alongside Lily Dempsey and Madame.

I could almost see Madame in front of me now – those icy blue eyes seemed to be hovering in the dark reflection of the glass, shining out of a face as wrinkled as a walnut . . .

'*Eek!*' For the second time that morning, my own voice startled me. It *was* Madame I was looking at. She was on the other side of the fire door, gesturing impatiently at me to open it for her.

I bolted to my feet and grabbed the handle. Madame buzzed through, then swung her chair round to face me. I dreaded to think what I looked like – out of the corner of my eye I could see curly clumps of hair that had sprung out of my hairnet, and I could feel that my headband was askew. I didn't have to glance down, either, to know that my tights were wrinkly round my ankles and my knees.

Stealthily, I curled my shoeless foot round the back of my other leg, and prayed Madame wouldn't notice the shoe itself, lying limply in the dust further along the corridor.

I held my breath while all these worries fizzed inside my head, and Madame fixed me with her uncomfortably hard stare.

'Luci Simpson,' she said at last. 'Do not lean over on your supporting leg when you *pirouette*.'

I looked at her, stunned, for a moment, before realising she must have been watching me through the glass door as I danced. How long had she been sitting there? The thought made me blush and shiver both at the same time.

'Pull up on your supporting side,' she continued. 'Here.' She stroked one gnarled hand up from her waist to her armpit, to demonstrate what she meant.

'Yes, Madame,' I said humbly.

'Well – show me!' she commanded.

I hesitated for a second, then placed my feet in preparation as before, trying not to notice how much the hand held out in front of me was shaking.

Thankfully, I managed the turn without falling over.

'Hmm,' Madame grunted. 'A little better. But do not fling your arms so hard. Use them strongly, yes, but if you fling them, they will knock you off balance.'

I nodded and swallowed and waited for her to ask what I was doing in the corridor. But all she said was: 'Now open the door for me.'

42

I ran to the swing door she'd just come through and opened it again.

'Not that one!' snapped Madame. 'The studio, of course! Be quick about it.'

In my haste, I flung back the door to Dempsey Studio so hard it banged on the wall. Then, not daring to glance in at Miss Latimer, I stood aside while Madame buzzed herself into the room.

I was dying to follow her in. What was she doing? She'd never visited our class before. After a moment, when the door had stopped swinging on its hinges, I bent my knees and squashed myself right up against it, so my eyes could just peep over the lip of the glass panel. I didn't want anyone inside to spot me.

Every girl in the class was standing in fifth position, knees pulled up, with a shining, eager look on her face that reminded me of my puppy, Rocket, when he thinks you're going to throw a stick for him. Madame was in the centre of the studio, and I could hear the murmur of her voice, though I couldn't make out what she was saying. Sometimes she looked over at Miss Latimer, who was standing by the piano, and Miss Latimer nodded and gave a simpering sort of smile. Mr Judd even smiled too.

I was just beginning to think that my legs had seized up and I'd be stuck in this funny half-crouch forever, when I saw Madame reach for the controls on her chair-arm and turn round to face the door. I ducked away from the window and grabbed the handle,

43

holding it open like those top-hatted doormen at posh London hotels.

Madame sailed past as if I wasn't there.

'Now, now, girls!' I heard Miss Latimer say as the door swung shut again. 'Don't get too excited. We have work to do.'

Ten

'What is it? What did Madame say?'

I flung myself on Sadie as everyone streamed out of the studio at the end of class, buzzing with excitement.

'A dream come true! I can't imagine it!' she said, her eyes shining. Then she clutched my arm anxiously. 'But I bet they won't choose me – oh—'

'What is it?' I cut in. 'What's happened?'

'The British National Ballet,' said Pippa, appearing with Ella at my other side. 'But I suppose you haven't heard of them?'

'Of course I have!' The BNB was only one of the most famous ballet companies in the world! But, of course, Pippa thought an Aussie wouldn't know that.

'Well, they're coming to the Grand Theatre for two weeks this Christmas—'

The Grand was in Wittingham – the nearest big town to our school.

'To dance a completely new ballet,' put in Ella.

'Called *A Christmas Carol*,' said Sadie. 'After that story by Charles Dickens – the one with Scrooge in it, you know?'

I nodded. Paul, who was my step-dad now (though he hadn't been then), had read it to me and Frankie last Christmas. We'd almost been sick laughing so

45

much at his impression of Scrooge, the grumpy old miser who hates having fun. It was an ace story.

'So what's happening?' I asked. 'Are we going to see it?'

'Better than that!' said Ella. 'We might get to be in it!'

'*In* it?' We'd reached the top of the changing room steps by now, and the three of them huddled round me, bouncing up and down with excitement. They were all talking at once.

'Mr Bell – that's the choreographer – told Madame he needed some children—' Pippa went on.

'And Madame told *him* she doesn't let first years take part in professional shows—' Sadie cut in.

'But he insisted he only wants the youngest pupils in the school. So she says she's going to let us this once—' continued Ella.

'Because the BNB's such an important company—' gushed Pippa.

'And we're all auditioning this Thursday—' Sadie squeaked, finally.

'The day after tomorrow?' I said.

They nodded.

'All of us? Me too? Even though I wasn't there?'

Sadie, Ella and Pippa looked at one another.

'Must be.'

'Don't see why not.'

'Miss Latimer can't leave you out.'

But I had to be certain. If there was the slightest, tiniest chance Miss Latimer was going to make me miss my chance to dance with the BNB I wanted to know about it!

I ran off along the corridor.

'Luci!' I heard Sadie calling after me. 'Where are you going?'

I knocked on the staffroom door, and then waited, my insides all jiggly with nerves and excitement. I could hear the low murmur of voices inside, but no one answered. After what felt like hours, I knocked again.

This time, the door flew open immediately.

'Well?' thundered Mr Edwards, fixing me with a challenging stare. He was quite old, but he still had a chest like a barrel, and a strong deep voice that boomed inside it like a church bell.

'Erm,' Mr Edwards' demanding look suddenly made me feel as limp as a dishcloth. 'Please could I speak to Miss Latimer?' I said.

Mr Edwards did not blink. 'You *could*, I imagine,' he pronounced, 'since you appear to have the power of speech. The question, I would have thought, small girl – ' (and from the way he said it you would have thought the word girl was an insult) ' – the question is whether you *may*.'

He baffled me with that one. As far as I was concerned it amounted to the same thing. I nodded and smiled as if I understood. 'Yes, Mr Edwards.'

Mr Edwards stared hard at me for an uncomfortably long moment, then turned his head, as self-consciously as if someone had asked him to show his profile. 'Miss Latimer?' he said, swirling the syllables round in his mouth.

'Yes, Mr Edwards?' I heard Miss Latimer say.

'There is a small girl requesting to speak with you.'

'Yes, Luci?' said Miss Latimer coldly, as she took Mr Edwards' place in the doorway.

'I'm sorry about class, Miss Latimer,' I began. I figured I had to get through this bit first. 'It was an accident. Honestly. I never meant to—'

'Accident or no, this is typical of what your conduct has been all term, Luci,' said Miss Latimer with a dismissive sweep of her hand. 'You do not listen to a word I say. You set a bad example.'

'I do try—' I began.

'Then you don't try hard enough!' cut in Miss Latimer with a steely stare.

'No, Miss Latimer,' I said, hanging my head.

'However,' Miss Latimer went on, her voice softening a little, 'I take your coming to see me now as evidence that you are still prepared to try and improve. That is good. Perhaps this half-term break will be an opportunity to start afresh, hm?'

'Yes, Miss Latimer,' I said. But then she began to close the door. 'Oh, Miss Latimer!' I put my hand out against it. 'One more thing!'

'Well?' Miss Latimer looked at me in irritation.

'It's the audition. The British National Ballet audition. Am I in it too?'

Miss Latimer gave an impatient sigh. 'You are,'

she said. 'Though in my view, there is hardly much point in every last child auditioning.' In the category of 'last children' she clearly thought I was the very last of all. 'But Madame has decided that it will be a useful experience for you.'

She looked at me, and must have seen the hopeful, delighted expression that had spread over my face.

'Oh, Luci!' she said, letting out a cold, tinkling laugh, like a crystal chandelier in a breeze. 'I wouldn't get your hopes up, my dear!'

As she shut the staffroom door, I was still staring up at the place where her face had been. I heard her rippling laughter recede into the room beyond.

It was then that I decided. I was going to show Miss Latimer once and for all. Show Sadie, Pippa and Ella, too – show everyone!

As I turned and broke into a run, my feet pounding on the corridor floor, carrying me away from Miss Latimer and her sneering looks, I was saying just one thing inside my head, over and over.

I *will* get a part, I *will* get a part.

Eleven

'If we have to do *sissones* tomorrow, I won't stand a chance!' said Sadie the next night, when the four of us had gathered in our bedroom for a last chat before lights out. 'Mine are dreadful. Especially those ones going backwards – I can't get the hang of them at all. Oh, I wish the audition was further away!'

'I'm glad it's not!' said Ella, who was taking up most of the floor space practising the splits. 'I can't sleep at night for thinking about it! I don't know whether I'm more scared or excited.'

'I wonder what the costumes will be like,' said Pippa dreamily. 'I do hope mine are nice. Of course, the Grand Theatre won't be anything like Covent Garden—'

'Pippa—?'

She frowned at me, puzzled by my pause. 'Yes? What?'

'Have you ever had an audition like this before?' I hated asking Pippa for advice, but this was no time to be stuck-up. The audition was too important to me.

'Of course. Lots of times,' said Pippa breezily.

'Well—' I hesitated again. 'What was it like? What did they get you to do?'

'Oh,' Pippa drew in a deep breath, and seemed to be searching for something to say. 'You know, different things . . . this and that . . .' She shrugged. 'You can never tell, really.'

'But – do you think he'll give us steps we haven't done before?'

'Who?' She looked puzzled.

'This Mr Bell!' Really, I was astonished by how dense Pippa could be sometimes.

'But Mr Bell isn't taking the audition,' said Pippa, as if *I* was the stupid one.

I looked at the others. Sadie nodded. 'Didn't we say? We're just going to have a normal class with Miss Latimer and Mr Bell's going to watch.'

It felt like someone had put a handful of ice cubes down my back.

'No!' I said, covering my face with my hands. 'Tell me it's not true!'

'Why, what's the matter with that?' said Ella gently.

'Everything!' I moaned. 'Miss Latimer hates me! Mr Bell's hardly going to be impressed when he hears her telling me off all the time, is he?'

'Well, there's a perfectly simple answer,' said Pippa briskly. 'I've told you before – it's your style Miss Latimer doesn't like. So dance her way for a change.'

'Do you think I don't try?' I blurted out. 'It works for about two steps – but then the real me takes over. I just can't dance like her!'

There was a miserable silence.

'Ah!' Suddenly Sadie bounced to her feet, as if

she'd just sat on a pin. 'That's it! Luci' – she grabbed my arm eagerly – 'do an impression of Miss Latimer for us.'

'Are you kidding?' I said. 'Look, I'm not in the mood right now.'

'Come on!' Sadie urged. 'You're great at impressions. And I've got an idea. Do her when she's demonstrating a step.'

'Well . . . OK.' Reluctantly I got up, and stood thinking for a minute, picturing Miss Latimer in my mind. Ella moved to make room for me.

I stretched one leg out to the front and, bending down, brushed my hand along it. 'And – forward bend, girls,' I intoned in Miss Latimer's voice. 'Gracefully – like a reed in the breeze. And come up – rise,' I went up on to the ball of my foot, 'and run to the corner.' With a faraway wistful look in my eyes, I drifted across the bedroom.

Sadie squealed with laughter. 'Perfect! I knew you could do it!'

'So – what use is that?' I said in my own voice again, turning round to face her.

'Don't you see? When you do an impression of Miss Latimer, you dance exactly the way she wants you to. So,' Sadie grinned at me triumphantly, 'do one long impression of her in the audition!'

Ella clapped her hands. 'That's a brilliant idea!'

'Sadie – get serious!' I shook my head.

'But the steps you did just then looked fantastic!' said Ella. 'And if that's what it takes to stop Miss

Latimer shouting at you – why not?'

'You honestly think it'll work?' I searched Ella's face for a hint of a giggle. This just had to be a wind-up! But she looked deadly serious.

'Definitely!' said Sadie. 'You'll be transformed into Miss Latimer's perfect pupil!'

'Make sure your clothes are neat, too,' said Ella.

'And what about putting your hair in a bun?' suggested Sadie.

'What – this mess?'

Pippa reached over and pulled at one of my curls. 'Hmm,' she said. 'I think it's just long enough. If we use plenty of gel and hairspray.'

'Hey!' I swatted her hand away.

'And hand over those ballet shoes of yours,' said Ella sternly. 'I'm going to sew the ribbons on so they *can't* come off!'

'OK, OK! I submit!' I laughed. 'Give me the full make-over!'

'I want to get started now!' said Sadie, bouncing up and down in excitement.

Just at that moment the door opened.

'How nice to hear jolly voices!' said Miss Lum, smiling in at us fondly. 'The rest of the corridor seems to be shaking with nerves about tomorrow. But you're taking a much better attitude, I can see. Well done, dear hearts!' She tapped her watch. 'Past lights out time, though, I'm afraid. Run along to your own room, you two.'

'Yes, Miss Lum.' Ella and Pippa got up and headed

for the door. Miss Lum stood back to let them through.

'Night-night all!' she trilled, shutting the door behind her. 'Sweet dreams!'

Part Three

The Perfect Pupil

Twelve

'All right, Year One,' said Mrs Baker, with an exasperated sigh. 'You may put your books away – *quietly* – and get your things ready for the audition.'

At long last the moment had come. Desk lids flapped and banged, nervous fingers zipped up bags and checked pockets for combs, brushes and headbands. Then we were on our way.

Guy Jenkins and his mate Alex Brodie plunged past us with an ear-splitting 'Nyyowwww! D-d-d-d-d!' and their arms outstretched, their rucksacks on their backs, doing their usual fighter-plane routine.

'Pathetic!' I heard Pippa muttering under her breath as they passed. 'I wonder if there are any parts for complete idiots in this ballet?'

'Come on, hurry up!' said Sadie. 'We've got to have time to get Luci ready!'

We raced across the lawn and down the gravel path

to the Dance Wing. It was drizzling slightly, so most of the others had gone the long way round, keeping indoors. But we were determined to bag some bench and mirror space.

'Right,' Sadie said to me when we'd clattered down the stairs to the changing room. 'We'll get ready ourselves first, and then get started on you. Put your tights and leotard on while you're waiting.'

'Right you are.' I opened my bag and took out my dance clothes. I'd even folded them properly – that had to be a record!

'Now,' said Ella a minute later, taking the last of her hairpins out of her mouth and prodding it expertly into her bun. 'Sit down. I'm going to tie your shoe ribbons for you.'

'And I'll start on the hair,' said Sadie. 'Come on, Pippa, give us a hand.'

Pippa was changed already, and had been admiring herself as she did a *port de bras* in the mirror. She jumped guiltily to attention. 'What?' she said. 'Oh, right.' And she sighed.

Ella slipped my feet into my ballet shoes, tied the drawstrings and tucked them under, and then tied the ribbons, criss-crossing them neatly around my ankles and tucking the ends – or 'pig-ears' – away out of sight.

'Not too tight?' she asked when she'd finished.

I pointed and flexed my feet a few times.

'Perfect!' I said.

Meanwhile, Sadie and Pippa were brushing my hair savagely and scraping it back to make a bun. I felt like a grand prix racing car in a pit stop, with a team of mechanics crawling all over me, fixing this and adjusting that.

'Stand back!' commanded Ella, picking up the can of hairspray. With one hand shielding my eyes, she sprayed my head all over.

Then Sadie and Pippa fell on me again, brandishing grips, pins and a hairnet that was so thick it looked more like a string bag.

At last, just as we heard Josie Wells say, 'It's three-thirty, everyone! We'd better get going!' Sadie, Ella and Pippa pronounced me finished.

I touched my fingers to my bun. It felt like a rock cake had been welded to my head – I could have gone out in a hurricane and I don't think it would have budged.

'Have a look!' Sadie urged me, and pushed me over towards the mirror.

I looked. And then looked again. I could hardly believe my eyes.

A girl with sleek, smooth hair was staring back at me; a proper, elegant ballet student. Her neck looked longer than mine usually did and, without the busy hair all round it, her eyes looked bigger too.

'Great job, guys!' I said, turning back to face them and putting my hands up for a high five. 'Thanks a million!'

Thirteen

I knew exactly what this BNB choreographer, Mr Bell, would be like. I could see him in my head: a stately-looking old man, with white wispy hair and a silk cravat. He'd stand up ramrod straight and fix me with his beady stare and say crisply: 'You, my dear, you have talent! I will make you a star!'

Thwump!

The studio door swung open and everyone in the room sucked in their breath.

But it was only Mary-Beth. She hurried in, looking a little red-eyed and sniffing slightly. Josie shifted along to make space for her at the barre.

Thwump!

The door went again.

'Good afternoon everyone.' This was it. I lifted my leg down from the barre, where I'd been stretching over it in a side bend, and stood to attention in fifth position.

'Good afternoon, Miss Latimer.'

Miss Latimer was looking really smart; she had a peach-coloured swishy dress on, plus an extra-long chiffon scarf trailing over her shoulders.

'I would like you to meet Mr Robin Bell from the British National Ballet.' Miss Latimer held out her hand.

I looked for the wispy-haired gentleman. But through the door came someone quite different. He was young, with ruffled hair that made him look like he'd only just woken up. He was dressed in trainers, jogging bottoms, and at least two scraggy sweatshirts, one on top of the other.

'Good afternoon, Mr Bell,' we all said together.

'Er – hi. Please call me Robin.' He beamed, running a hand through his hair. 'Right, Daphne.' He glanced at Miss Latimer. 'Shall I sit here?'

Daphne? I'd never really thought of Miss Latimer having a first name, let alone one like Daphne. I caught Sadie's eye, but she was too nervous to giggle.

Miss Latimer smiled graciously and nodded.

'So, girls and boys. *Pliés* — '

As Mr Judd struck up the first few chords, I saw Miss Latimer glance my way and do a double take, just as I had when I'd seen myself in the changing room mirror.

I held my head up proudly. After a moment's hesitation, Miss Latimer nodded, then turned away.

For the whole audition, I imagined myself as Miss Latimer. Instead of bounding, I glided. Instead of stretching, I wafted. I thought of feathers and flowers and summer breezes. It was as if I'd left the regular Luci Simpson down in the changing rooms with my school uniform.

I tried skimming over the floor. I made my arms

59

drift through the air, and did little extra wafty movements with my hands like I'd seen Miss Latimer do sometimes. I imagined myself in a swishy skirt, with a chiffon scarf round my neck.

And it worked. Like a dream.

'Good girl, Luci!' Miss Latimer exclaimed in an unmistakeable tone of surprise. 'That's much better.'

I carried on with my *ronds de jambe*, hoping this Robin guy wouldn't hear how shocked Miss Latimer sounded. But I figured, not having sat in class before, he probably wouldn't notice.

By the end of class, when Robin asked us all to sit on the studio floor, I was wafted-out. I couldn't have pictured another fairy or misty morning if I'd tried.

'I've really enjoyed watching you all,' Robin was saying. 'And what I'm going to do now is go away and have a really hard think. Then, in a couple of days, I'll let Daphne know who I've chosen.'

There was a shuffling as everyone sat up straighter in a last attempt to make him notice them.

'What I'll need,' he went on, 'is two teams of kids who will take turns at performing. That's because there are laws about how many hours you can work in a week.

'The biggest child's part in this ballet will be a character in the story called Tiny Tim.'

I groaned – and so did most of the girls. It *would* have to be a boy's part!

But Robin saw what we were thinking. 'I don't necessarily need to cast a boy in the role,' he said, laughing. 'Tiny Tim wears a cap, so a girl could easily hide her hair.'

A hand waved. It belonged to David Wilder, the smallest boy in our year.

'Please,' he said, 'does it need to be the *tiniest* person playing Tiny Tim?' He was looking hopeful.

Robin laughed again. 'Not necessarily. Just a really good dancer! Oh – and one more thing,' he said. 'The show runs at the Grand for two weeks, ending on Christmas Eve. So, unless you live near here, I'm afraid you won't be able to go home for the holidays till late Christmas Eve night—'

'Which means spending the first week of the Christmas holidays here, at school,' Miss Latimer said.

There was a gasp, followed by a peculiar silence as everyone let this thought sink in.

Miss Latimer spoke again. 'We shall of course be writing to the parents of those of you who get parts, to ask their permission to keep you for the extra time in school. However, if anyone knows straight away that they will have a problem with this, please see me afterwards.'

No one did go up to see her, of course, though the thought of spending half the Christmas holidays at school was pretty horrendous. But as we poured out of the studio and back along the corridor, even *that* couldn't take the smile off my face. The plan had worked. More than worked – it had been ace. Mum, Paul and Frankie could book their tickets. I was a dead cert for the show.

Fourteen

'If the audition results aren't up by the time Daddy arrives, I won't go,' declared Pippa, as we queued for Saturday lunch. 'I can't bear it – not knowing all half-term!'

'My mum's going to be here at two-thirty,' said Sadie. 'And I don't think – oh no, not peas *again* – I don't think she'll want to hang around.'

'Daddy won't either, but he'll just have to!' said Pippa, picking through the cutlery basket for a clean fork.

'And what if the results don't go up today at all?' I asked. 'Will you make him stay overnight too?'

Pippa couldn't see I was joking. 'No,' she said seriously. 'I'll make him complain to Miss Stretton – or Madame herself!'

We went through the kitchen door and into the dining hall. Just as we had chosen a table and were putting our trays down there, I spotted a figure hurrying between the chairs towards us.

'Hello, folks!' Shona greeted us cheerily, putting down her tray next to Pippa's. Pippa didn't look too pleased. 'Ready for the off, then?'

'You look very cheery,' said Ella. 'I thought you were dreading half-term?'

'Was I?' Shona looked puzzled.

'You said last week – your mum always buys too much fattening food.'

'Oh yes!' Shona began picking the croutons carefully out of her soup and leaving them in a little heap on the side of her plate. 'I've solved that one!'

'How?'

'Sucking a lemon,' said Shona gravely.

'What about it?'

'Helps stop you feeling hungry – it's the perfect solution! No matter what food there is in the fridge at home, if I'm not hungry, I won't want it, will I?'

'Youch!' My tummy was hurting, just thinking about it. 'Lemon juice on an empty stomach sounds awful! Who wants not to feel hungry anyway? It'd spoil the fun of eating.'

'It really works!' said Shona, taking no notice of me. 'I did it yesterday. I skipped lunch and didn't feel hungry at all. I mean, could you skip a whole meal?' She seemed to be asking Pippa this last question.

'No problem,' said Pippa confidently. 'I skipped lunch yesterday too, as it happens.'

I knew this was a lie. I'd seen Pippa eat lunch with my own eyes.

'Did you?' Shona looked a little disappointed for a moment. Then she looked down at her tray. 'Ah – forgotten a spoon! Back in a sec!'

'You didn't really skip lunch, Pippa,' whispered Sadie when Shona was out of earshot.

Pippa shrugged. 'I know. But Shona boasts so much, I can't let her get the better of me, can I?'

I smiled. Funny old Pippa. Sometimes I almost felt proud of her.

Just then there was a kerfuffle at the door to the dining hall. Josie Wells was standing there, panting, and Mary-Beth, Guy, Alex and Vaz Khanduri were clustered round her, talking eagerly.

'Looks like the notice is up,' I said, feeling suddenly rooted to my chair.

'Oh!' Pippa was on her feet. 'I'll just go and check it.'

And she was gone, slipping between the chairs at the tables and joining the stream of girls and boys heading off towards the corridor.

A second later Shona was back, spoon in hand. 'I asked Pippa to look for me too,' she said. 'I can't bear to go myself! Golly!' She rubbed her stomach. 'Nerves really take the edge off your appetite, don't they?'

Sadie, Ella and I looked at one another and said nothing. I think we were all holding our breath.

After what seemed like an age, Pippa appeared in the doorway, a beaming smile on her face.

'She's got a part, anyway,' I muttered.

'Well!' Pippa flounced back into her seat, and leant forward confidingly. Then she paused, enjoying the rest of us hanging on her every word.

'Spit it out!' I shouted. 'You're in – but what about us? Hey?'

65

'We're *all* in!' said Pippa. 'And in the same team too!'

'Yes!' I shouted, jumping on to my chair and punching the air with my fist. 'We've *done* it!'

I felt so happy it was like a firework display had gone off in my head. I'd shown Miss Latimer! I *was* as good as the others!

'Luci Simpson! Get down immediately!'

'Sorry, Mrs Sykes.'

I clambered back into my seat, and Sadie, Ella, Pippa and I held hands across the table, still trembling with excitement.

'Me too? Me too?' Shona was asking desperately, plucking at Pippa's sleeve. 'What about me?'

Pippa turned and looked at her, and suddenly seemed almost reluctant to answer. 'Yes,' she said, with a sour look. 'You're in our team too, Shona. You're Tiny Tim.' She said the words as if they left a nasty taste on her tongue, then turned back to the rest of us.

Shona was speechless for a moment, eyes wide, mouth open. Then she put a hand to her forehead, and her smile changed to a frown. 'Oh no!'

'What?' Pippa looked at Shona eagerly, as if she was hoping Shona had just realised she couldn't do the show after all.

'*Tiny* Tim!' Shona almost wailed. '*Tiny*! Just look at me! I must lose weight before the rehearsals start!' She prodded her tummy and her thighs. 'Here, and a bit here and here, too. I wish I had loads of money.

Then I could go to one of those plastic surgeons over the holidays and have it all sucked out!'

Sadie pushed away her plate of food, looking a little green.

'For goodness' sake calm down,' said Ella. 'They've given you the part, haven't they? You're fine as you are.'

But Shona hardly seemed to hear her. 'I must have a lemon! I must have one right now! I'll go and ask Cook.' And, scraping back her chair, she stood up and hurried off in the direction of the kitchens.

Shona didn't appear again for the rest of lunch, and, when we'd finished, I took her discarded tray as well as mine back to the washing-up point in the kitchens.

Outside, the four of us linked arms, and skipped down the corridor like Judy Garland on the Yellow Brick Road. As we rounded the first corner, we came face to face with Miss Latimer.

'Congratulations, girls,' she said, stroking her chiffon scarf like she was preening her feathers. 'I can see from your faces that you know the results of the audition.'

I beamed at her. I wanted her to congratulate me in particular – to admit she'd been wrong.

As if by magic, Miss Latimer did turn to me. 'And I'm glad to see you're not too disappointed, Luci. That is a very good attitude to take.'

Disappointed? I didn't understand.

'But I've got a part too, Miss Latimer,' I said,

thinking she might not have read the list correctly. 'In the same team as the others.'

'Of course you have,' she said, smiling indulgently, 'in a manner of speaking. Understudies do have a vital job to do, after all.' And she swept on past us with a laugh and a final, 'Congratulations!' called over her shoulder.

I turned to Pippa. 'Understudy? You never said . . .'

Pippa was biting on one fingernail and frowning. 'Oh – now I come to think of it, there *was* a little "u" next to your name. I wondered what it meant.'

I felt like a snake had wrapped itself round my insides and was squeezing really hard.

'Luci—' Pippa began.

'I'm going to look at the list,' I said, pulling my arm free of Sadie's grasp, and heading off down the corridor.

An hour and a half later, I was sitting on Sadie's case. It's got a dodgy catch, and someone always has to sit on it or it won't do up.

'Got it!' she said, as I heard a click. 'OK, you can stand up now.'

I checked out of the window again. 'What colour did you say your car was?'

'Blue. It's a Maestro – that's sort of square-ish, like a lump of chocolate.'

'Yep – one's just coming down the drive now.'

'Let's see!' Sadie squeezed in beside me to get a look. 'It's them! I'd better go down. Oh – Luci, give me a hug!'

'Have a great week!' I said.

'You too.' Sadie stood back and looked at me. Then, with a smile, she shook her head. 'I'm so impressed, you know. If *I'd* been cast as an understudy I think I'd have been really upset. But you've been brilliant! I really admire you!'

'Thanks.' I suddenly found I had to swallow hard to stop myself blubbing. I wanted to fall on Sadie's shoulder and tell her how awful I felt, but after what she'd just said, I didn't reckon I could.

So I waited till she'd gone. Then I checked both ways along the corridor, to make sure Miss Lum wasn't on the prowl, shut my door again, buried my face in my pillow, and sobbed my eyes out.

Part Four

On With The Show

Fifteen

'It's just a rock'n'roll *lurve* song –
Specially for my bab*e e e*!'

As the car rattled over the gravel, Mum was singing along with the radio at the top of her voice. Her head bobbed from side to side, and her purple papier-mâché earrings swung like they were in a hurricane.

Usually, I would have been joining in, but right now my heart had sunk into the bottom of my sneakers, and my voice felt like it had slid there too.

Just a few short weeks ago, when Mum had driven me to school for the beginning of term, the sight of the red-brick tower pushing up jauntily through the trees had thrilled me. The whole building had seemed friendly – I thought the windows in the tower had looked like eyes, smiling down at me in welcome.

Now, on my way back after the most miserable half-term of my life, the school had completely changed. At the bottom of the tower, the entrance archway was a yawning mouth, and for a second as we went under it, I felt I was being swallowed whole, like Jonah getting eaten by the whale.

Mum's bracelets jangled as she pulled on the steering-wheel, crunching the car round into a parking space in the courtyard. She yanked on the handbrake and turned the engine off. The radio cut out in mid-wail.

'Well,' said Mum, turning to look at me. 'Here we are, honey. Give me a hug.'

'Grrrlmph,' I said into her shoulder.

'Listen.' She pushed a curl out of my eyes. 'Remember what Paul said, OK? He was an understudy loads of times before he started breaking through into the big roles. And now look at him – film scripts plopping through the letterbox every other day. He'll be in Hollywood before we know it!'

I smiled. 'Yeah, I know. But acting's different.'

'Are you sure?' said Mum. 'I don't think so. You may not have been right for this show, but you'll be spot on for another, you wait and see.'

'It's not just the show, Mum,' I said, fiddling with one of the buttons on my school cape. The thread was wearing thin – it'd fall off soon, I noted absently. 'I'm not sure I want to stay at the Evanova.'

'What?' Mum looked at me like I'd just landed from Mars. 'You want to quit?'

'Yes. No. Oh—' I turned my face to the window. Outside this bright red car with multi-coloured Mum at the wheel, everything looked drab and cold and miserable. 'I tried my best in that audition,' I said, watching my breath make a misty patch on the window pane, 'and I still didn't get a part. So that must mean I just haven't got what it takes to be a dancer.'

'Rubbish – it's just one audition!' exclaimed Mum. 'Look, honey, you begged to come here, remember? And you loved it straight off. What about those friends you told me about? Ellie, Poppy and – what's the other one's name?'

'Ella, Pippa and Sadie, Mum.'

'That's it! What about them, huh?'

To be honest, I couldn't even picture saying goodbye to them – it was too awful an idea. But now I just shrugged. 'Sure I'll miss them. But I don't want to be the hanger-on in the gang, Mum.'

'Hey, hey, hey!' Mum leant over and pulled at one of my curls gently, then let it spring back into place. '*My* Luci? A hanger-on? I don't believe it!'

I said nothing.

Mum sighed and sat back in her seat. The purple earrings swung against her neck. 'OK, honey. See how you go for the rest of this term. If you still feel the same at Christmas, we'll talk about it then.'

Christmas.

What a Christmas it was going to be! Only getting home late on Christmas Eve, when all the best things would have happened without me: the tree decorated, the tinsel up, all those exciting shopping trips over and done with. And what was I missing all that for? For the frustration of watching everyone else have the time of their lives performing with the BNB. The thought of it made me feel sick.

'Then the night before last we had a box at Covent Garden,' Pippa said proudly. 'For *Coppelia*. It was quite good, though Mummy said she thinks Marla Anderson is past her prime.'

'I'd love to go to Covent Garden,' sighed Ella, pulling her dressing-gown tighter around her.

'And on the other nights Mummy and Daddy went out to dinner parties,' Pippa rattled on. 'Something with the Prime Minister, and something at the French Embassy.'

'Did you get to go too?' Sadie, unable to get into her bed because Pippa was sprawled on it, was perched on her locker, wiggling her bare toes and looking at Pippa in awe.

Pippa shook her head. 'Dinners like that are terribly boring, Mummy always says.' She raised one leg up towards the ceiling and pointed her foot. 'But she told everyone about me being in *A Christmas Carol*!'

'My dad couldn't stop talking about it all the time I was at home,' said Sadie. 'And he took us all out for a special meal to celebrate.'

Ella grinned. 'You lucky thing!'

'And Miss Cole, my old dancing teacher, rang to say she'd be coming to see the show,' added Sadie. 'So did Mrs Winter.'

'That's the woman who danced with Madame when

she was young,' added Ella, in case we'd forgotten.

'You know – the one I told you about who used to teach me piano?' said Sadie. I nodded, and she carried on. 'Anyway, she said that dancing with the BNB was going to be the best possible start to my career!' She giggled at this, half in embarrassment and half in delight.

Then Ella looked over at me. 'You're quiet tonight, Luci,' she said. 'You've hardly said a word about your half-term. How was it?'

'Oh – really great,' I said.

The three of them looked at me, expecting more. But I couldn't think of anything to say. What was I going to tell them about? The row I'd had with Frankie just because she'd rearranged our bedroom furniture without asking me? The way I'd moped around all week, wondering whether I should give up ballet for good?

I picked at the fringe on my bedspread. 'Really,' I said, trying to sound enthusiastic. 'Just great.'

Sixteen

'Oh, it's so thrilling, girls, I feel quite ready to faint! But look – ' Miss Lum pulled off one mitten and rummaged in her large carpet-bag. 'I come prepared!' She brought out a small book with 'Autographs' written in gold letters on the cover. 'I've got forty-three dancers' signatures in here, going right back to 1962 – and there's room for plenty more!'

'Have you got Margot Fonteyn's?' asked Melanie Cooper eagerly, jigging from foot to foot to keep herself warm.

Miss Lum shook her head. 'I had a chance to get hers in 1965,' she said. 'But I missed her – on account of my rain-hood.'

Rain-hood? Sadie and I glanced at one another and raised our eyebrows. 'How come?' I asked.

'Oh, my dear! It was such shocking bad luck!' Miss Lum looked grief-stricken at the memory. 'I'd been waiting for hours at Covent Garden stage door in the pouring rain, when, all at once – poof! – a gust of wind broke one of the strings on my rain-hood and sent it flapping off down the street. Well, naturally, I ran after it. And when I got back to the stage door, Miss Fonteyn had gone.'

'How sad,' said Sadie.

'Tragic,' agreed Miss Lum. She pulled out a large

embroidered hanky and dabbed at the corners of her eyes.

'Miss Lum, the coach is here,' said Ella, pointing to the end of the driveway, where a big green West's Travel Bus – For Private Hire, had already pulled up and was waiting.

'Why, so it is!' said Miss Lum, pushing back her hair and looking flustered. 'And I haven't even counted heads yet! Gather round, children! Quickly!'

It was Wednesday afternoon, and everyone involved in *A Christmas Carol* had been let out of History early, in order to be bussed into Wittingham for the rehearsal. Miss Lum was chaperoning us, though she seemed far too excited herself to be in charge.

'Will there be real dancers there?' asked Sadie breathlessly, as Miss Lum hurried us towards the coach. 'Grown-up ones?'

'Of course there will,' said Pippa.

'I wonder if we'll actually get to dance with them,' said Ella. 'I hope they'll be friendly.'

'Hurry, hurry!' Miss Lum stood by the coach door, whirling her arms like an orchestra conductor to try and get us up the steps more quickly.

'Bags I don't dance with Josie Wells,' came Guy Jenkins' loud voice from far down the coach, where he'd elbowed his way through to claim the long back seat. 'She smells!'

'I wouldn't dance with you, Guy Jenkins, if they paid me!' shouted Josie from somewhere behind me, as I spotted four spare seats together and made a lunge for them.

'So, d'you reckon I'll have to learn everyone's part?' I asked, when we were sitting down, and the coach had finally pulled away on to the long road into town.

Sadie and Ella looked at Pippa, since she seemed to know the answer to everything. Pippa shrugged. 'All the girls parts, I should think. And – who's the boy understudy in our team?'

'David Wilder,' I said.

'David, then, will have to learn all the boys' parts,' said Pippa. 'Mummy says being an understudy is all hard work and no reward.'

What little cheeriness I'd been feeling suddenly evaporated. 'Thanks,' I said sarcastically. 'That makes me feel heaps better.'

'But at least you're in the team!' said Sadie quickly. 'I mean – you're coming to the rehearsals and everything. Just think how horrid it would be if you weren't involved at all!'

'Still sitting in History with Mary-Beth,' nodded Ella.

'Yeah, right,' I said. 'I'm lucky to be an understudy, is that what you're saying? I should feel grateful, because really I'm not good enough even for that?'

With a horrified look, Sadie blurted out, 'No! It was just bad luck you didn't get a proper part! It could have been any one of us!'

I shook my head and turned to look out of the

window at the houses and gardens flashing past. It had started to rain.

In the gap between the window pane and the seat in front, a slice of Pippa's face appeared. 'Look, Luci,' she said huffily. 'It's not *our* fault you're an understudy, is it? Why do you have to take it out on us?'

'I am *not* taking it out on you!' I shouted.

Ella frantically put her finger to her lips. The hum of chatter on the coach seemed to have died down all of a sudden, and several heads were craning above their seat-backs to see what was going on.

'Anyway,' I hissed more quietly, 'if I wasn't made an understudy because I'm not as good as you lot, what was the reason? Hm? Miss Latimer even said I was dancing better. What more could I have done?'

'Behind every prima ballerina is a *corps de ballet*,' said Pippa sagely. When she saw the looks Ella and Sadie shot her she spread her hands and shrugged. 'Well? It'd be no use if *everyone* was brilliant, would it?'

'Perhaps you're just—' began a voice above me. I looked up, startled, to see Shona leaning over from the seat behind.

'Just what?' I said crabbily.

'You know,' said Shona. 'The wrong shape. If you went on a diet—'

'Oh shut up, Shona!' I said, turning to face the front again. 'Who asked you anyway?'

Out of the corner of my eye, I caught sight of Sadie

79

looking at me nervously, as if she'd just found herself sitting next to Miss Stretton, instead of Luci Simpson.

I counted to ten, took a deep breath and put a hand on her shoulder. 'Look,' I said, trying to sound a bit more normal. 'Forget it. I'm sorry. I don't mean to spoil things for you.'

Sadie smiled at me gently. 'You're not,' she said. 'I just wish you had a part too, that's all.'

The rehearsals weren't being held in the theatre, but in a large hall on the far side of Wittingham. When the driver had parked in the street outside, Miss Lum stood up in the gangway at the front of the coach, a hand on the seats on either side of her.

'Now, dear hearts,' she began. 'I know we're all terrifically excited, but we must remember we are representing The Evanova School at this rehearsal. We must be on our best behaviour, mustn't we?' She smiled round brightly. 'Good! Well, off we go! Don't leave any of your belongings behind. And don't push!' she added, as she spotted Guy and Alex throwing themselves out of their seats at the far end.

'It's those last few chords – *pam-pam-pam-PAM*! Can we have them just a tiny bit slower, so the girls can make it on to the boys' shoulders? Oh – hi kids!' Robin flashed us a grin as we filed into the draughty hall. Beside him, the pianist took a pencil from behind his ear and made a note on the music.

In the centre of the room, about thirty-five men and women were talking, laughing and getting their breath back. You could tell instantly that they were dancers. They stood so straight it looked like they'd had a broom-handle sewn into their clothes, and their feet, even now they were relaxed, were splayed out sideways, like elegant ducks.

'Just dump your bags in a corner, kids,' said Robin, nodding towards the back of the room. 'I'll be with you in a second.'

He clapped his hands to get the grown-up dancers' attention. 'OK, people. Let's go from the top one more time.'

The dancers took up their places, and the pianist started to play.

'Don't they look weird?' Sadie whispered in my ear, as we got out our ballet shoes and sat on the floor to put them on. I nodded.

The couples whirled; the men lifted the women high in the air and set them down again, steadied them as they spun in *pirouettes*, then launched into the air themselves and twizzled round several times before coming down to land. Some of the couples went wrong, and swore, or shot Robin a worried look, and on a lift, one of the women overbalanced and ended up coming back to earth in fits of giggles.

But the dancing wasn't the weird thing. It was what the dancers were wearing. I'd only ever seen real dancers on stage before in fantastic costumes made of net and lycra and sequins. This lot looked like they'd all been to a jumble sale and just thrown on the first clothes they'd found. There were baggy old

T-shirts, sweatshirts with rips and frayed edges, plastic trousers that looked like several bin-liners sewn together, and mouldy old leg-warmers that would've given Miss Latimer a fit just to look at them.

Of course, Pippa was the only one of us not surprised.

'Oh, dancers always wear clothes like this,' she whispered.

'I suppose when you get to wear such beautiful costumes on stage, it must be a relief to look a mess sometimes,' whispered Ella.

'A bit better, people,' Robin said when the music had stopped. 'You're still a whisker off the timing at the end there. And Ed and Laura – you'd better sort yourselves out, darlings, or I'll have to re-cast you. Now,' he turned towards us. 'All ready, kids? Let's have a look at you. Team A over there' – he pointed to one side of the room – 'and Team B the other side.'

I hesitated, then stuck up my hand.

'Yes?' Robin frowned, as if he hadn't time for questions.

'Understudies too?' I asked.

'Hm? Oh – no, darling, no. Understudies, sit and watch for the moment. I need to see how many bodies I'll have on stage. But watch carefully,' he added sternly as David Wilder and I, along with Melanie Cooper and Vaz Khanduri, the Team B understudies, headed for the spare chairs at the front of the room.

'You'll need to learn all the dances. I'll let you have a go later. OK?'

Two hours later we still hadn't danced a step. In fact, the only time Robin had remembered the understudies existed was when David and Vaz had started tussling over David's *Space Zone* puzzle book, and he'd bellowed at us all to shut up, and go and practise in the corner if we couldn't sit still.

So we jumped up and down amongst the bags for a while. But trying out steps on your own that are meant to be danced weaving in and out of lots of people on a crowded stage isn't much fun. Soon we were sitting down again, watching the others.

'Josie – you little idiot!' screamed Robin the next moment, rapping on the piano lid to stop the music. 'How many times have we been through that sequence? You're getting in the way of Adam' (that was one of the grown-up dancers) 'and he's having to go round you every time. How he still comes in on the beat for the start of his solo I don't know. Get it right, girl.'

Josie promptly burst into tears. But Robin took no notice.

'All you kids should know this is a professional production,' he said stonily. 'Not some amateur fiasco. And if you're going to perform like professionals you need to concentrate like professionals. Now – let's try it again, shall we?'

As I watched Josie stumble through another run-through, I couldn't help thinking, surely, *surely* I wasn't worse than that? But, then, why had Josie got a part and not me?

The question just wouldn't go away. And there was only one person who knew the answer.

Seventeen

'OK, that's it for today!' said Robin at last. 'Thanks, everyone!' The grown-up dancers gave a little round of applause – a bit like doing curtsies for your teacher at the end of class, I suppose – and Robin slipped off his ballet shoes and stuffed them in his big battered hold-all. I could see Miss Lum hovering nearby with her autograph book. Robin had spotted her too, but he was trying to pretend he hadn't.

This was it. The moment of truth.

Without giving myself time to chicken out of it, I bounded up from my seat, ran over and tugged at the hem of Robin's sweatshirt.

'Yes?' He turned round to me, just as Miss Lum made a lunge with her pen and book. She backed off again sheepishly.

For a moment, with Robin looking at me so matter-of-factly, I had to squish my hands together really hard to stop myself from running away.

'Excuse me, Robin, but why—' I hesitated, then ploughed on. 'Why did you only make me an understudy?'

He looked at me for a moment, and an expression of utter amazement lit up his face. Then he half-laughed, as if he was embarrassed, and rubbed his chin.

'Well,' he began. 'If you really want to know . . .' He glanced at me doubtfully.

I nodded.

'You did dance well,' he said. 'But your dancing was very lyrical. Do you know what that means?'

'Sort of.' My throat had gone dry. I gave a little cough. 'Sort of airy-fairy?'

Robin laughed. 'I wouldn't have put it quite like that, but yes – that's about the size of it. And dancing like that is fine,' he added hurriedly. 'Daph – er, Miss Latimer danced very much in that style herself and I know she encourages it in her pupils. It's exactly the right style for lots of ballets. Just not for this one. I was looking for more attack, more energy – nothing pretty-pretty, d'you see? Don't let it worry you though – it's just a question of—'

'Mr Bell? Could you possibly?' Miss Lum was getting desperate. She'd crept up on the other side of Robin and was now waggling her autograph book under his nose.

'Ah – of course.' Robin smiled at her wearily, then turned back to me. 'Look, we've all been understudies at one time or another. It's a good chance to watch other people's mistakes and learn from them. You'll have your chance in the next show, I expect. Don't let it get you down.'

And with that, he took Miss Lum's pen and book and turned to her saying, 'To?'

'Oh! Lilian, please,' said Miss Lum breathlessly. 'That's L-I-L—'

For a moment I stood exactly where I was, my mouth open, catching flies, as my little sister Frankie would say. Then I ran over to the corner to get my belongings.

'What was that all about?' asked Sadie, as we slung our bags over our shoulders and followed the others out of the hall.

'Tell you on the coach,' I said.

'Well?' said Sadie, when we were sitting down and Miss Lum was going along the aisle counting us for the millionth time, as the coach driver revved up the engine.

Pippa and Ella were managing to peer both at once through the gap between the seats in front – one eye each. They'd seen me talking to Robin too.

'I asked him why he'd only made me an understudy,' I said, pulling the pins out of my bun, and shaking out my hair so that my curls sprang back into place. I wasn't going to bother with *that* palaver any more.

'You *what*?' gasped Pippa and Ella.

The two eyes between the seats – one blue and one dark brown – grew large as saucers, and Sadie let out a nervous giggle.

'You heard,' I said. I couldn't keep a grin off my face.

'And what did he say?' gulped Sadie.

'Well,' I dumped the hairpins in my bag and zipped it up again. 'He said that I *had* danced well at the audition, but that he didn't pick me because, out of

87

everyone, I was the most lyrical dancer. That means airy-fairy,' I added, for the benefit of Sadie, who was frowning. 'He said he knew that was how Miss Latimer liked people to dance, and that it was a good style for a lot of ballets. But for this ballet, he wanted more energy, more attack, more—'

'More like the way you usually dance,' said Sadie quietly.

'Exactly!' I exclaimed, slapping my knee. I beamed round at my friends.

But Sadie, to my astonishment, promptly burst into tears.

'What's up? Sadie?' I tried to prise her hands away from her face.

'It's – all – my fault!' she spluttered. 'It's my fault you haven't got a part!'

'Not just you.' Ella knelt up in her seat and put her chin on the headrest. 'All of us.'

'What – me as well?' said Pippa, appearing beside her and looking put-out.

'Of course,' said Ella evenly. 'We persuaded Luci to dance the way Miss Latimer wanted at the audition, didn't we?'

'And that's why she didn't get a part!' wailed Sadie.

'But don't you see?' I said. 'This makes it OK. I thought I hadn't got a part because I was hopeless at ballet. That's why I've been so miserable – I was even thinking I ought to give up dancing altogether! At least now I know Robin thought I danced well. More than that: I know that if I'd danced the way I usually

88

do – the way I *like* to dance – I'd be in the show!'

'What difference does it make? You still haven't got a part.' Sadie brought out a paper tissue from her pocket and blew her nose, hard.

It may sound silly, but in all my relief and excitement at what Robin had said, I hadn't fully realised that, as far as *A Christmas Carol* was concerned, nothing had changed. For a moment that sinking feeling pulled at my insides again. But then I had an idea.

'Hey – Robin'll probably notice me at rehearsals,' I said, warming to the thought even as I said the words. 'When I get to do some dancing, he'll spot me and realise that I'm perfect for the show after all. Then he'll just have to find a part for me!'

I grinned round at my three friends. Somehow, though, they didn't look convinced.

Eighteen

Pas de basque to the right, *pas de basque* to the left; heel and toe and *pas de bourrée*.

I loved this scene. It was the street scene in Act Three, when Scrooge, the grumpy old man, has been changed by the three Christmas ghosts into the jolliest old man in the world. He looks out of his window (for the moment, Jeremy, the dancer playing Scrooge, just stood on a chair at the back of the stage area) and watches the people going past: children running errands, or having snowball fights, men and women rushing in and out of shops, stopping to chat to each other and laugh and joke and wish each other a very merry Christmas – just through their movements, of course, as you don't get speaking in a ballet.

The music was jaunty and the steps Robin had choreographed for the kids to do were great: fast and lively and based on real-life actions, like running, skipping and leap-frogging.

'Is that one *pas de basque* or two?' Melanie whispered to me.

'Two the first time, then one the second time and run to the corner.'

'Oh, yes, I remember.'

David, Vaz, Melanie and I had found a space at

the back of the hall to practise. It was tough keeping up with all the different steps Robin was teaching to different people, and my head felt fuzzy with trying to remember everything at once.

But there was one little dance I'd got just right. Amelia Parker, who was in Team B, was having problems with it – she was still trying to do it as Miss Latimer would have wanted, and Robin was nearly tearing his hair out.

'No, Amelia, *no*! Get some oomph into it! You're supposed to be having a snowball fight, not auditioning for *Swan Lake*.'

Amelia bit her lip and tried again.

Look at me – look at me – I tried to telepathise to Robin. I knew exactly what he wanted. I'd got the steps perfectly, and if he would only glance my way I could show him.

I tried the sequence again, edging forward as I did so into the space just in front of Jeremy's chair.

'You – understudy!' I heard Robin's voice call as I finished the last *pirouette*. This was it – he'd noticed me! He'd seen how good I was at the dance – how much better I was than Amelia.

'Yes?' I said eagerly, stepping forward.

'Keep out of the way, will you?' said Robin, flapping his hands to send me back again. 'You're really confusing things. I'll only let you practise at the back if you keep well away from the main action. I don't even want to notice you're there. OK?'

'Oh – OK.' I nodded glumly and slunk away.

So much for my great idea. I looked like I was stuck with just being an understudy after all.

Nineteen

'Look – the new rehearsal schedule's up!' Sadie ran over to the noticeboard and peered at a large sheet of white paper with the school crest stamped at the top.

'Only one more week to go – I bet we've got rehearsals every day. And there's that English project to hand in too!' Ella was looking worried.

'Oh, I'm not going to bother with that,' said Pippa.

'Really?' Ella looked shocked. 'But Mr Bronan will be furious!'

'So what?' Pippa shrugged. 'It's his fault for expecting people involved in a professional production to have time for his silly projects. What use will First World War poetry be to me, anyway, when I'm grown-up and dancing Aurora in *The Sleeping Beauty* every night, eh?'

'But, Pips,' I said, 'what if you don't make it as a dancer? What if you have to think of another career?'

Pippa frowned for a moment in puzzlement. Then she pushed me playfully and laughed. 'Oh, you're such a joker, Luci!' she said. 'For a moment there I thought you were serious! You really do say the silliest things!'

'Rehearsal hall . . . rehearsal hall . . . Grand Theatre . . .' Sadie traced her finger down the list.

'Why do we only go to the theatre on Sunday? It hardly gives us any time to get used to the stage. The show opens on Tuesday.'

'It's because there's a different show performing there this week, and they only finish on Saturday,' said Pippa with a sigh, as if it was perfectly obvious. 'Then the stage crew spend all Saturday night taking down the old set—'

'All night?' said Sadie. 'They must get so tired.'

Pippa nodded. 'And then we start rehearsing there on Sunday.'

'Sunday.' Sadie found the place on the rehearsal list again. 'Team A – that's us. "Technical rehearsal", it says. What's that?'

For once, I jumped in with the answer before Pippa could.

'It's when you do a run-through for the theatre technicians,' I explained. 'My step-dad has to do them when he's in a play. He says they go on for ages, because you're always stopping and starting while they alter the lights, or work out problems with scene changes.'

'You have to be in costume, too, so that they can check everything looks right,' added Pippa.

'Oh, great! I can't wait to wear mine!' said Sadie.

Pippa shrugged. 'The "tech" is a dreadful bore. I wish our team wasn't doing it.'

I looked over Sadie's shoulder at the list. Team A had the tech on Sunday and then the opening night on Tuesday. Team B was doing the dress rehearsal on Monday, and then the second night on Wednesday. This was so that both teams would get the chance for a run-through on stage before they had to perform for a proper audience.

'At least it means we get to do the first night,' Ella reminded Pippa. 'That'll be really special.'

'Mmm,' said Pippa. 'I suppose so.'

'Well, I don't know what you're all squabbling about,' I said, putting on a miserable expression. 'Tech, dress rehearsal, first night, second night – I wish I could do any of them!'

'Oh, I'm sorry, Luci,' said Ella, putting a hand on my arm. 'I forgot.'

I looked at her sorrowfully for a moment, then broke into a great big grin. 'Ha, ha! Made you worry!' I crowed, slapping her on the back.

'You—' Ella began, but I cut her off.

'Come on, guys, let's get to the dining hall. It's chips tonight – I can smell them from here. Last one in the queue's Miss Stretton's pet!'

And I hurtled off along the corridor to make sure it wasn't me.

Twenty

The Grand Theatre in Wittingham is as white and smooth as a giant lump of cream cheese. There's a fancy iron canopy on the front and, below that, a whole row of glass doors, like the entrance to a big department store. The middle door's the best – it goes round and round and you have to jump in just at the right moment, like in a skipping game.

By the time our school coach pulled up outside the theatre at ten o'clock on Sunday morning, two men with ladders were already taking down the notice on the canopy that said, '*Snappity Snap* – the Hottest Musical in Town!' Down on the pavement lay the new strip: 'The British National Ballet,' it said, '*A Christmas Carol* – World Première.'

'We're going backstage in a real theatre,' said Sadie, squashing her nose against the coach window. 'Oh, I can't wait!'

Our chaperone today was Mrs Pondswell, the junior boys' matron. She was really grumpy, with a face that looked like she'd taken Shona's advice and sucked too many lemons.

'Hurry up everyone!' she snapped, as Team A tumbled off the bus on to the pavement. 'No dawdling! Follow me!'

I was surprised that, while the front entrance looked so smart, the stage door of the Grand Theatre was really shabby. It was just a small white door with peeling paint, halfway down a dirty alleyway.

'Stage doors always look grotty,' said Pippa. 'It's practically a tradition in itself.'

Mrs Pondswell led us inside. In a narrow entrance corridor we met a man with thinning grey hair and a pot-belly wrapped up in a bottle green cardigan.

'Morning, morning,' he said with a grin, rubbing his round stomach and nodding to us.

'All right, Henry?' a young man called to him, pushing against the tide in a bid to get out.

'Can't complain,' Henry replied.

'Who's he?' I heard Sadie whisper to Pippa.

'The door man,' said Pippa, making no effort to keep her voice down. 'He decides who can come in and who can't. I remember at one of Mummy's performances, there were so many fans at the stage door, the door man nearly got flattened!'

Henry had a tiny office which opened off the corridor. Its walls were covered with signed photographs of the famous people who'd performed at the Grand.

'Wow!'

'Darcey Bussell!'

'And there's Lily Dempsey – see!' came the gasps as we crowded round, spotting all the familiar faces.

Henry chuckled. 'Could be you, one day!' he said.

'Could be?' said Pippa. 'Will be, more like!'

'Team A! Stop wasting time and follow me!' snapped Mrs Pondswell.

With a sigh, we left Henry and his tiny office behind.

At the end of the corridor was a hallway, with whitewashed walls and a cold concrete floor. There was no furniture except for a ragged sofa with half its stuffing spewing out, and several massive wicker hampers.

Sadie looked a little crestfallen. 'Not very glamorous, is it?'

'This is where the star's dressing-rooms are,' Pippa was explaining to anyone who was listening. 'They always get the rooms nearest the stage.'

One open doorway led off into darkness. A notice beside it said: 'Stage – Prompt side.' Straight ahead of us was a wide stone stairway curling up to the next floor on one side, and down on the other. On the down side, another notice said, 'Under-stage passage – to Opposite Prompt.' It all looked very confusing.

As we climbed the stairs behind Mrs Pondswell – passing one floor, then another, and another – from time to time figures rushed past us: dancers in dressing-gowns with half made-up faces, or people all in black – black jeans, black pullovers, black Doc-Martens.

'Stage-hands,' nodded Pippa as they went past.

'They look like they're going to a funeral,' said Shona, puffing up the stairs just behind us.

'It's so they don't get seen so easily in the wings,' said Pippa.

'Oh, yes, I know *that*,' said Shona quickly. But I could tell she didn't.

We carried on climbing till the staircase ran out. The top landing was much like all the others we'd passed: square, concrete-floored and bare-looking, with several doors leading off it. Mrs Pondswell headed towards one of them. On it was pinned a small card.

The Evanova Kids.

The second Mrs Pondswell opened the dressing-room door, it was like a game of musical chairs when the music stops, as everyone rushed for a seat in front of the mirrors.

'I got here first!'

'No you didn't! This one's mine!'

'Rachel, Rachel – sit here, look!'

'Stand up again – all of you!' barked Mrs Pondswell, planting her hands firmly on her hips. 'What do you think you're doing? Behaving like a bunch of ruffians!'

There was a scraping of chairs, and a rustling, then silence.

'Now – this partition' – Mrs Pondswell pointed to a high screen that ran down the centre of the room, splitting it into two narrow sections – 'is to divide the boys' side of the room from the girls' side—'

'Thank goodness!'

'Don't want to sit with the boys – they're *stupid*–'

'*Quiet!*' roared Mrs Pondswell. 'I do not want to see any of you crossing over to the wrong side of the room at any time without my permission. Now, find a seat sensibly, while I come along and give you your make-up boxes.'

'Thank goodness we're not going to be cooped up with Mrs Pondswell all day,' I said to David, as we picked our way along one of the empty rows of seats. The auditorium seemed really dusty and echoey with hardly anyone in it. 'How do you lot stand her?'

David sat down and shrugged. 'Pondsnail's not so bad, really. She is a bit strict, though – silence after lights out, making your bed neatly, that kind of thing.'

'I can imagine.'

Robin had sent a message to say we could watch the tech from the front, but during a real performance, David and I would have to sit in the dressing-room. I didn't fancy spending three hours a night with 'Pondsnail'.

'Brian, that spotlight's in the wrong place,' came Robin's voice over a crackly microphone. 'Sort it, will you?'

I turned round in my seat. Robin was in the middle section of the stalls, about halfway back, with a woman and a man I hadn't seen before. There was a big board in front of them, making a table over the top of the next row of seats. On it were two microphones, and loads of buttons and switches.

Worried-looking people were running up and down the aisles, bringing messages to Robin, or to the little room right at the back of the auditorium where the controls for the lights were. Occasionally, a dancer drifted on to the stage, thickly wrapped up in jumpers and leg-warmers, and then drifted off again. I sat back down in my seat.

After what seemed like an age, Robin bent towards the microphone again. 'OK, people. Let's get started.' Then the lights went down, and the ballet began.

'The costumes look ace!' whispered David.

'And the make-up,' I said. 'Look at Jeremy!'

At rehearsals, I'd never been able to picture Jeremy as Scrooge. Scrooge was supposed to be old, and Jeremy was young. But now, when he came out on stage, I gasped. He really did look as if he had a thousand wrinkles crammed on to his forehead and cheeks.

'The lights downstage right look horrendous!' shouted Robin, and the pianist, who was standing in for the orchestra, stopped in mid-bar.

There were more scurryings and whispered conversations. The dancers on stage stood about with their hands on their hips.

'OK. Go again!' Robin shouted.

All the stopping and starting was frustrating to watch – though it must have been worse for the dancers. Still, no one complained.

'There's Shona!' I nudged David. We'd both had

to learn Tiny Tim's part. 'I love this first dance she gets to do.' And I waggled my feet on the floor in time to the music, going through the steps of the dance.

I had to admit it: Shona was very good. For much of the ballet, Tiny Tim's supposed to be ill and frail – and Shona managed to look so delicate you really did get the impression she could collapse at any moment.

Robin didn't seem so impressed with her, though. When at last they got to the finale, which was a carnival with all the characters in the ballet dressed as animals (this was Robin's idea; it wasn't in the original story, and Pippa said she thought it was 'terribly vulgar'), Shona didn't come on when she should have done.

'Stop!' said Robin into his microphone. 'What on earth's going on?'

Nervously, Shona crept out from the wings.

'I – I couldn't get changed into this costume quickly enough,' she explained, holding up the mouse mask that she should have been wearing.

'Then change by the side of the stage and get someone to help you,' Robin snapped.

'Er – Mrs Pondswell is already helping the boys round the other side.'

'Well then get someone else!' Robin shouted. 'For goodness' sake, we can't keep the audience waiting for you, can we?'

'No.' Shona hung her head, and looked relieved

when, a moment later, Robin turned his attention to some problems with the scenery.

Later, in the coach on the way home, Shona tapped me on the shoulder.

'Luci – will you help me with that quick change?' she asked.

'Sure,' I said. 'You'll have to tell me what to do, though.'

'I'll show you on Tuesday night,' said Shona. 'Thanks.'

Twenty-one

Mr Bronan, on breakfast duty in the dining hall, was giving out the post.

'Jenny Koutsoudi,' he called in a bored voice, and flapped a long blue envelope in the air as a third year girl hurried between the tables to collect it from him.

'You've lost how much?' asked Ella, chasing the last cornflake round her bowl.

'A kilo,' said Shona. Her eyes shone with pleasure. 'But that's just since last Monday. I've lost loads this term altogether.'

'Martin Saville,' droned Mr Bronan.

'You do look thinner,' said Sadie, chomping a big bite out of her toast and marmalade.

'I should think so!' Shona said proudly. 'The wardrobe mistress at the theatre was really cross because she'd made my costume to fit the measurements they took at the audition – and it's too baggy for me now.'

'Pippa Parnell-James—'

I looked at Shona. Sadie was right – she did look thinner. But more than anything, she looked pale and tired. There were dim blue shadows under her eyes, and she had quite a few spots on her chin and forehead. I couldn't believe she thought slimming made her look *better* – but I hadn't the heart to say anything.

'Pippa Parnell-James!' shouted Mr Bronan. 'How many times do I have to say it before you wake up, girl!'

'Me?' Pippa jumped to her feet, dropping her spoon clattering on to her tray. 'A letter?' She darted off towards Mr Bronan, who was glaring at her and looked ready to rip the letter into bits.

A moment later, Pippa was back at the table, her cheeks flushed with delight. 'It's from Mummy!' she said, as she sat down again.

'What – a whole letter?' I teased her, licking my finger and dabbing at the crumbs on my plate. 'Not a postcard with three and a half words on it, like normal?'

Pippa glanced up haughtily as she tore at the envelope. 'Mummy and Daddy usually have to go to far too many important meetings and functions to have time to write whole letters.'

'Yeah, well, my mum doesn't have time to go to important meetings and functions,' I replied, putting on Pippa's voice. 'She's too busy writing to me!'

Sadie giggled, but Pippa took no notice. 'I wonder if Mummy and Daddy are going to bring any famous directors to see the opening night tomorrow?' she said eagerly, unfolding the paper.

She scanned the letter. But suddenly, her expression changed. Her teeth fastened on to her lower lip and her chin began to tremble.

'What is it?' asked Ella. 'Is something wrong?'

Pippa looked up, and her eyes were brimming with tears. 'They're bringing some directors,' she quavered. 'But on Wednesday, not tomorrow, because that's when some of Daddy's important business friends are going.'

'But it's a Team B performance on Wednesday!' said Sadie.

'I know.' All the usual haughtiness in Pippa's manner had disappeared.

'You mean they aren't coming to see you at all?' I asked her.

Pippa picked up the letter again, and was quiet for a moment, reading. Then she nodded. 'They're coming on Thursday – by themselves.'

'Ah, there you go!' I said, leaning back in my seat. 'That's not too bad – your second performance!'

'But I wanted them to come to the *first* one!' exclaimed Pippa crossly.

I shrugged. I couldn't really see that it made much difference.

'Mummy says–' Pippa began, her voice catching, 'that I shouldn't mind, because it's not as if I've got the main part or anything.'

'Well, that's true,' I said. 'Tiny Tim's the–'

'But don't you see?' Pippa snapped, screwing up the letter in her hand. 'If I had the main part, she would have made the effort to come on the first night! This is her way of telling me I'm – I'm not doing well enough. She's disappointed in me.' Pippa hung her head, and tears plopped down on to the table. Ella put an arm round her shoulders.

I could hardly believe anyone's mother could be so mean. At least I knew that, if I'd had a part in the show, Mum and Paul would have dropped everything to be there.

'Hey!' I said, trying to think of something cheering to say, 'It's a good job you're not an understudy like me!'

Pippa looked up with a watery smile. 'Yes,' she said. 'You're right. That would have been *really* dreadful. Mummy probably would have given up on me altogether!'

Gee, thanks! said a voice in my head. But for once I didn't let Pippa know how tactless she was being. I figured that perhaps things weren't quite as easy for her as I'd always thought.

Twenty-two

'Luci – can you do me up?'

'Is my lipstick all right?'

'My petticoat's showing! Luci, can you come and pull it up at the back?'

'OK, OK!' I shouted. 'One at a time!'

At the theatre on Tuesday night, I was so much in demand to help with costumes and make-up, I didn't have a single moment to feel left out. It was just as well – I wished so desperately I could go on stage too, that I probably would have cried.

'This is your fifteen minute call,' came the voice over the tannoy. 'Fifteen minutes please.'

'I've forgotten all my steps!' cried Rachel Cooper in an agonised voice. 'Every last one!'

'Nonsense, dear girl!' said Miss Lum confidently. 'They'll come back to you as soon as the music starts.'

'Luci?' I heard a voice behind me.

I did up the last hook and eye on the back of Sadie's dress, patted her shoulders to let her know I was done, then turned around. Behind me stood Shona – already in her Tiny Tim costume, with her hair tucked inside her Victorian boy's hat. She was holding another jacket, a pair of trousers and the mouse mask: her costume for the finale.

'These are what I need for that quick change. Can

you bring them down to the wings when it's time?'

'Sure,' I said. 'But I don't know where to go.'

'I'll show you.' Shona asked Miss Lum for permission, then led me out of the dressing-room and down the flights of stairs to the hallway by Henry's office.

'Opposite prompt is the side of the stage you'll need to be,' she said. 'So you'll have to go down these stairs to get across.'

I followed her down the long, shadowy corridor that passed beneath the stage. It was stacked with old chairs and boxes and bits of broken scenery, like a junk shop, and lit by two bare lightbulbs dangling from the ceiling.

At the far end of the corridor, we came to another short flight of steps leading up – and at the top I found myself standing in the wings at the side of the stage. The noise of the audience – the chatting, the rustling of programmes and the banging of seats as people stood up and sat down again – was very near here, but because the curtain was still down the normal lights were on and it wasn't too dark. Stage-hands and grown-up dancers were milling about, talking through scene changes or trying out steps. Tucked in one corner of the wings I noticed a box of rosin, and some of the women dancers were queueing up to rub the soles and ends of their pointe shoes into the powder, so they wouldn't slip on stage.

'Here.' Shona led me right to the front of the wings. 'If you stand well back in this corner, I'll run off through this gap in the scenery here' – she pointed – 'and you can help me change straightaway. OK?'

'No worries!' I said. It seemed simple enough.

'It was great – I didn't do a single thing wrong!'

'Must be the first time ever, then, Josie—'

'You trod on my toe! After the *pas de basque*, we go right first, not left!'

'Did you see Jeremy? He stuck his tongue out at Simon when he had his back to the audience!'

When Team A careered back upstairs just before the interval, it sounded as if the first half of the show had gone really well.

'Now, now!' Miss Lum clapped her hands. 'Simmer down girls and boys, please! Thank goodness we're on the top floor – if we were any closer to the stage the audience wouldn't be able to hear the orchestra for all your fuss.'

'How was it?' I asked Sadie, Ella and Pippa as they came in, panting and grinning.

'Fine,' said Pippa.

'Brilliant!' said Sadie and Ella together.

'Were you nervous?'

Sadie looked at Ella and giggled. They both nodded. 'Terrified!'

'But it's like one of those really scary roller-coaster rides,' said Sadie. 'As soon as you get off, you just want to do it again!'

There was a knock at the door and Robin stuck his head round.

'Well done, kids – you're looking good!' he said. 'But keep well back in the wings when you're waiting to go on – just because you can't see the audience, it doesn't mean they can't see you. Remember, please!'

And with that, he was gone.

'Have you got everything?' asked Shona anxiously.

'Jacket, trousers . . .' I counted through the things on my arm, '. . . and mask. All here.'

'Great,' said Shona, hurrying to the door. 'I'll see you down there, then.'

If the interval had passed in a flash, the second half of the show had gone even quicker. Now Shona had just gone downstairs for her last scene before the finale.

Clutching her costume tightly in case I dropped something, I followed Miss Lum to the ground floor. She had a bundle of costumes as high as her chin.

'Lord bless me!' she gasped. 'I never thought this job would involve dressing half a dozen children in the dark!'

In the hallway we parted company, Miss Lum heading off to the prompt side wings, and me going down the steps to the junk-filled corridor.

For a moment, as I looked along its dimly lit length, filled with strange shapes and shadows, I felt nervous. I quickened my pace to a trot and hummed under my breath.

The next second there was an almighty clattering of footsteps ahead, and four grown-up dancers hurtled along the corridor towards me.

'Out of the way, little one!' panted the man in front.

I flattened myself against the wall, and saw a flash of sweat-drenched faces as they rushed past me. Then I peeled myself off the wall again, hurried along the corridor, and took the steps up to the wings two at a time.

It was dark. For a moment I stood still, blinking to get used to it. The only light came from the stage – which looked dazzlingly bright. Through a gap between two scenery flats, I watched the dancing. It was odd to see a performance so close up. The dancers were all side-on to me, facing out to the audience, with smiles on their faces as if to say: this is no effort at all! But, the minute they'd bounded off-stage in a beautiful *jeté or brisé*, they'd be doubled up with their hands on their knees, gasping for breath, and complaining of the pain in their feet, or legs, or back.

'Move, move, move!' hissed Jeremy. I hadn't seen him coming, and he rushed off-stage so fast I had to dart away to avoid him crashing into me. I hurried over to the dark corner at the front of the wings where Shona had told me to stand. From there I could see her on stage too, looking just as confident of her steps as the grown-ups. She was doing well.

Pas de chat, soutenu turn, *pas de chat, pas de chat* – and Shona was running towards me, into the wings.

I was ready – I'd put the clothes down beside me so that I could help her undo her buttons. There was no time for modesty; as the other dancers rushed off-stage past us, she had to pull off her clothes as fast as possible, and I handed her the new ones to change into.

'The trousers, the trousers!' whispered Shona urgently.

Where had I put them? I turned back to where I'd left the pile of clothes, but they weren't there. Had someone kicked them out of the way by mistake? I peered into the shadows this way and that.

Then at last I spotted them. They'd got shoved up against the end of one of the scenery cloths.

'There!' I whispered, reaching out to grab them. But, just at that moment, the lights changed for the beginning of the finale, and the cloth flew up towards the ceiling, as the technicians changed the scenery. The trousers, dangling from the wooden baton that weighted down the bottom of the cloth, flew up with it, past my fingers – up, up and out of reach.

'No!' I cried, and I think the audience would have heard it if the cymbals hadn't crashed right at that moment, drowning out my voice.

I heard a thump behind me. It sounded like someone tripping over and falling heavily. I spun round. Shona was lying in a heap on the floor.

'Are you OK?' I shot over to her, to see if she was hurt.

But as the lights came up on the new scene on stage, I saw that Shona's eyes were shut. She couldn't hear me. She'd fainted.

Twenty-three

'Shona! Shona!' I hissed, patting her cheeks, gently at first, then quite hard.

The music had started for the finale, and the first dancers leapt on to the stage.

'Quick – you're on any second!'

Shona tried to push herself up on her arms, but then sank back again.

'I – I feel dizzy,' she whispered. 'I can't—'

I thought furiously. Shona had an important part in the finale. They couldn't do it without her – it just wouldn't work.

I looked around. The trousers for Shona's new costume were dangling up above our heads, but her old trousers were in a heap beside her, and her new jacket and the mask were there too.

Quickly, I hooked my hands under Shona's armpits, and dragged her back a little, so that she was leaning against the wall.

'Will you be OK here?' I whispered.

Weakly, Shona nodded.

I glanced to the stage. I knew from the music that Shona's entrance was very soon now. Hurriedly, I reached for the jacket, pulling at the buttons on my school blouse with my other hand.

My fingers were trembling. 'Blast it!' I hissed under

my breath, as one of my blouse buttons burst off and skittered into a dark corner.

I had no time to get Shona's tights. I put the trousers on over my bare legs, and grabbed the jacket. Luckily, it had only four big buttons to do up. Then I pulled Shona's ballet shoes off and shoved my own feet into them. I winced; they were a size too small – but they would just have to do.

As the notes for Shona's entrance sounded from the orchestra, and I saw Jeremy on stage glance over to the wings anxiously, I pulled on the mouse mask and rushed out into the dazzling light.

When I'd dreamed of getting the chance to go on stage, I'd always imagined how carefully I would prepare for it; I'd imagined how it would feel to stand in the wings collecting my thoughts, and listening for my cue.

But now, without even thinking about it, I was out on the Grand Theatre stage, dancing in the world première of *A Christmas Carol*.

I'd never even been through this scene with all the other dancers, but as soon as I heard the music, it carried me along. My legs just seemed to know the steps without me even thinking what they had to do.

As we took our bows at the end, the applause was deafening. I loved the sound. I drank it in. Part of this is for me, I thought – the audience liked my dancing! Never mind Miss Latimer, never mind not getting a part – the audience had seen my dancing and they liked it!

As the curtain came down for the last time, and the dancers gathered up the flowers that had been flung on to the stage, I rushed off into the wings.

'Hey!'

Immediately a hand gripped my arm and yanked me sideways, through a doorway I'd not seen before.

It was pitch black for a second, but then the light was flicked on. I pulled off the mask, and saw I was in what looked like a prop store cupboard, with Shona standing before me, pale, but much recovered.

'Quick!' she urged. 'Change back and give me those clothes – here's your school uniform. No one must know it wasn't me out on stage!'

'But you're ill!' I said.

'I'm not ill,' Shona snapped. 'It was nerves, that's all – or, or the heat of the lights or something. Come on, Luci, *please*! They'll be wondering where we are.'

I struggled out of the costume and back into my school uniform. Then, with the mouse mask tucked under her arm as if she'd just that moment taken it off, Shona led the way back up the stairs to the dressing-room.

Behind the door marked The Evanova Kids, it was mayhem.

'I saw my mum! Second row back on the left-hand side.'

'Mine waved! It was so embarrassing!'

'Did you hear the cheering? They loved it!'

'Settle down, dear children, please!' cried Miss Lum, looking rather tearfully proud herself. 'You've done a wonderful job tonight, but the coach will be here soon, and I must have you back at school before eleven! Oh – there you are, you two,' she said, spotting Shona and me. 'Wherever did you get to? Hurry up, now, hurry up!'

Five minutes later, most people were out of their costumes and swabbing at their make-up with big blobs of cotton-wool.

There was a knock on the door.

'Well done!' exclaimed Robin, coming in with the biggest smile on his face I'd ever seen. He had red smudges all over his cheeks from lipstick kisses. 'You did a very good job, Team A, and I just hope you can keep this standard up for the rest of the run!

'And Shona,' he added, placing a hand on her shoulder. 'The finale was fantastic! I've never seen you dance so well before. Marvellous stuff!'

'Thanks, Robin!' Shona murmured with a smile. But as Robin turned away, I saw her shoot me a guilty glance.

Twenty-four

'Sadie – are you awake?'

We were both in bed, and though the light had been off for a while, I couldn't sleep. I stared into the darkness in Sadie's direction, but all I saw was the outline of a shape under her duvet.

'Mmmm?' came her drowsy voice. 'What is it?'

'You know the finale tonight?'

'Ye-es?'

'Well,' I took a deep breath. I couldn't hold it in any longer; I just had to tell someone – or I was going to explode. 'That wasn't Shona dancing. It was me.'

There was a moment's pause. Then, Sadie, suddenly completely awake, said sharply, '*What*?'

'It was me. Shona fainted while I was helping her change. She came round pretty quickly, but she was just too groggy to go on – so I did instead.'

There was a scuffling noise, then Sadie flicked on her bedside light. She rubbed her eyes and looked at me.

'Why didn't you say? Why didn't you tell Miss Lum – and Robin?'

'Shona asked me not to,' I said. 'She begged. I guess I don't blame her. If Miss Lum knew she'd fainted she'd probably send her to sick bay and she might have to miss the next performance.'

'But it's so unfair!' Sadie exclaimed. 'Didn't you hear what Robin said to Shona about the finale? He said she'd never danced so well before . . . and it was *you*!'

'I know.'

'Wow.' Sadie scratched her head, taking it all in. Then she smiled – 'Hey, you got to go on stage then, after all!'

'Yeah,' I nodded. 'I should be glad, I guess. But you know what you said about being on stage feeling like a roller-coaster ride? When you come off – all you want is another go?'

Sadie nodded.

'Well,' I said. 'I reckon you're right.'

'Five seconds, six seconds, seven seconds – there goes another one!' Pippa pointed at me and laughed.

'What are you doing?' I said crossly, pulling at my tights to get rid of the wrinkles and taking my place at the barre. I checked the clock: Miss Latimer would be here any moment.

'Timing your yawns!' laughed Pippa. 'You haven't stopped ever since breakfast!'

'Yeah, well,' I said. 'I didn't sleep much, OK?'

'You'd better not let Miss Latimer see you yawning, then,' said Pippa. 'She'll have a fit.'

'Probably will anyway,' I muttered.

As it turned out, I was about right. Miss Latimer was in a particularly sour mood that day.

'Back to your old bad habits, I see, Luci,' she said,

coming up to me in the middle of *battements frappés* and flicking a finger at my hair disdainfully. I had it in a hairnet again, instead of gelled and sprayed back into a bun.

'Yes, Miss Latimer,' I murmured obediently.

'And in your dancing too, I've noticed,' she added. 'I *did* think you were improving just before half-term. But it seems I was wrong, after all.'

If only she'd heard what Robin said about my dancing last night, I thought! It just wasn't fair.

But all I said was, 'Yes, Miss Latimer,' again, and stared straight ahead of me as she walked away.

'*Grands battements en cloche*!' Miss Latimer called out a moment later. 'Do you remember what we did last week, girls? Prepare the arm to second and the leg *derrière* – then swing: one and two–' She broke off. 'Are you quite all right, Shona?'

'Yes, Miss Latimer,' came Shona's voice from further along the barre. I looked down the line – I could see Shona's hand gripping the wooden rail as if her life depended on it.

'You look somewhat pale, all of a sudden,' said Miss Latimer. 'Are you–'

'I'm fine!' Shona's voice had a note of strangled desperation. 'It's just the . . .'

Her words faded away. I looked round to where she stood – in time to see her knees crumple, and her whole body slump to the floor, knocking into her neighbour Mary-Beth, who staggered back and landed on her bottom.

'Quick!' Miss Latimer cried, running across the studio. 'Someone fetch Dr Payne! And for goodness' sake stop snivelling, Mary-Beth!'

'All right now?' Gingerly, Dr Payne helped Shona to her feet. 'Do you think you can walk with me to sick bay?'

'Yes,' Shona said, as Dr Payne clasped her round the waist.

'Let's see how we go.'

Miss Latimer held the studio door open for them as they left, and then returned to stand by the piano.

'Right, girls, let's—' She glanced at the clock. 'Oh dear, so very little time left. I think we must just have your *révérence*. Come into the centre quickly.'

As we did our curtsies – for once not standing in our usual rows – I saw Sadie trying to catch my eye in the mirror, but I couldn't make out the message she was trying to get across.

'Stand up very tall,' Miss Latimer commanded as the last reverberations of Mr Judd's playing died away. 'And – rest. Well, I will see you tomorrow morning, girls. Class dismissed.'

I ran straight over to Sadie.

'What is it?' I asked.

'Why not ask her?'

'Ask who? What?'

'Ask Miss Latimer if Shona being ill means you're on stage tomorrow night,' Sadie said.

'I'm not asking *her*.' I glanced over to Miss Latimer and made a face.

'Look, Robin's not here. And I don't expect you fancy knocking on Madame's door, do you?' Sadie went on.

'No fear!'

'Well, then! Who else is there to ask?'

She had a point. And if Sadie was dying to find out whether I was going to have the role – I wanted to know *twice* as much.

'Miss Latimer?'

She turned round with a smile but, seeing who it was, her face hardened. 'Yes, Luci?'

'I was just wondering – if Shona isn't very well, will I be taking her place, since I'm one of the Team A understudies?'

Miss Latimer looked at me, her lips pressed together. Then she said, 'Were you the only one told to learn the role of Tiny Tim?'

'Er – no. David learnt it too.'

'So I thought,' said Miss Latimer crisply. 'Mr Bell will have to choose between the two of you.' She smiled. 'Thank you for making me think of it, Luci. I shall remember to tell Mr Bell that I strongly recommend he does *not* choose you. I have heard from Mr Edwards that David is a talented dancer who works hard. I cannot say either of those things about Luci Simpson.'

She turned aside, busily putting the register away, and then checking her hair in the mirror.

I wanted to pummel on her back and scream, 'You're horrible to me! It's not fair!'

But I didn't. I ran for the door and slammed out of the studio.

When I told Sadie what Miss Latimer had said, she stopped in the middle of brushing out her hair and looked at me, horrified.

'But that's *awful*!'

'Sure is.' I was sitting on the changing-room bench, hardly making any effort to get ready, even though the room was quickly emptying as other first years hurried off to the School Wing for this morning's English lesson. Ella and Pippa had already gone ahead, scared of being late.

'You go too, don't wait for me,' I said to Sadie.

She seemed lost in thought for a moment. 'What? Oh – sorry, I was miles away.'

'I said you go too – I'll be along in a minute. You know what Mr Bronan's like if people aren't there on time.'

A strange look crossed Sadie's face – sort of half-excited. 'Yes, OK then,' she said suddenly, reaching for her bag. 'I'll see you in the classroom.' And, quick as a flash, she bounded up the stairs.

I sighed. Despite what I'd said, I'd rather hoped she'd wait for me anyway. 'Go on, then,' I muttered sulkily to myself under my breath as I stuffed my feet into my school shoes – the laces, as usual, were already tied. 'Leave me on my own. See if I care.'

'And what sort of time do you call this, Luci?' snapped Mr Bronan, scowling at me from his place by the black board.

I looked up at the clock on the wall. 'Erm – ten twenty-two,' I said.

There was a snort.

'Button it, Jenkins!' barked Mr Bronan. Then he turned back to me.

'Luci, you can write an essay,' he said, 'for tomorrow, entitled: Being Late. I shall expect you to hand it in at morning break. I would advise you not to be late with *that*.'

'Yes, Mr Bronan,' I mumbled, sliding into my seat.

I was so busy telling myself for the zillionth time how unfair life was that it took me a moment to notice something odd: Sadie wasn't in her usual seat next to me. Pippa and Ella were there all right, at the desks in front, but no Sadie. And she'd left the changing-room before me.

Five minutes later there was a knock on the door.

'Yes?' said Mr Bronan testily.

'Sorry, Mr Bronan,' Sadie panted, closing the door hurriedly behind her. 'I – I had to—'

'You had to be late, did you?' said Mr Bronan sarcastically. 'Don't even bother to make up an excuse, Sadie. Luci will tell you the title of the essay. Now – Wilfred Owen . . .'

'Where were you?' I said at break, when Sadie and I

had groaned together at the idea of an extra essay for Mr Bronan.

'When?'

'When you were even later than I was for English?'

'Oh!' Suddenly Sadie was staring intently at a tree over on the other side of the playground. 'I – had to carry some books for Mrs Sykes.'

'Right.' I scuffed my heels against the wall we were sitting on. 'Then,' I looked at her sharply, 'then why didn't you tell Mr Bronan? He would have let you off the essay.'

Sadie looked blank for a moment. Then she slapped me on the hand. 'Tag!' she shouted, jumping down and starting off across the tarmac.

'Sadie?'

'You're it!' she laughed. 'And I bet you can't catch me!'

Twenty-five

I could hear a funny rattling sound.

'Is that your teeth?' I said.

'Sorry!' David Wilder smiled. We were standing together in the corridor outside Madame's apartment. 'It's just – I'm terrified!'

'Why?' I said crossly. I shouldn't have been so crabby with him, but I just couldn't help myself. I knew Madame had summoned us about Shona's part in the show, and I knew that David was going to get it.

'Seeing Madame!' David shuddered. 'She gives me the heebie-jeebies!'

Before I could reply, the door in front of us opened and Miss Featherstone, the school secretary, emerged.

'You may go *in* now, children,' she said, whispering respectfully as if she was in church. 'Madame is ready to see you.'

David pushed me in front of him, so I went through the door first.

I would hardly have known it was the same room as the one I'd seen at the beginning of term. With cold afternoon sunlight replacing the red glow of the lamps, there was no sparkle from the gold-framed mirror, and the old books on the shelves looked dusty and unmagical.

Madame was sitting in her chair beside the empty fireplace. David and I stood to attention side by side, a few paces in front of her.

'Luci Simpson,' she said, looking at me, 'and David Wilder.' She shifted her gaze, then paused. Even if you didn't feel nervous before you went in there, Madame's way of looking at you without saying anything soon had you jittering.

'I have summoned you here on the grave matter of Shona Farley's health and her part in the current British National Ballet production.' Madame paused again.

'It seems,' she continued at last, 'that Shona will not be able to dance tomorrow night – or indeed on any night for the rest of the run.'

Before I could stop myself, I blurted, 'Is she very ill?' A horrible picture of Shona in hospital surrounded by tubes and machines had flashed into my mind.

Madame shook her head. 'She will recover. But it will take some time.'

I was desperate for her to explain more, but she paused again, then said, 'I believe you have both learnt the role of Tiny Tim?'

'Yes,' David and I said together.

'So Mr Bell has had to decide between you.' Madame nodded to herself. 'I have spoken to him today, and he has requested that Tiny Tim tomorrow night should be danced by . . . Luci.'

I gasped. I couldn't believe it. Had I heard wrong?

For a moment I thought I had, as I turned to David and saw a smile light up his face. But then Madame said:

'Luci, you must be aware that it is a very great responsibility. The audience must not suspect that you have taken over the role at short notice. The reputation of The Evanova School is on your shoulders. No one – least of all me – will forgive an inadequate performance.'

'No, Madame,' I said eagerly.

'And you should know,' went on Madame, 'that if, at any time during the run, Mr Bell considers you are not dancing well enough, he will call upon David to take your place.'

'Yes, Madame.'

'Go now.' Abruptly, Madame buzzed her chair round and proceeded away from us, towards the far door.

Out in the corridor, David and I both breathed a sigh of relief.

'Glad that's over!' he said, wiping his sweaty palms on his blazer.

I patted his shoulder. 'I'm sorry, David,' I said.

'What for?'

'You know – that I got the part, not you.'

'Are you kidding?' David grinned at me. 'I was praying I *wouldn't* get it.'

'How come?' The boy has to be nuts, I thought.

David looked at me guiltily. 'I never really bothered to learn Tiny Tim's part properly,' he admitted.

'There was so much else to take in and, somehow, I just presumed that one would never come up. Blimey, am I relieved!'

I laughed. 'Me too! I'm glad I don't have to feel sorry for you!' Heading off down the corridor, I turned left, and expected David to follow. But he didn't. 'Come on!' I called back, stopping to wait for him.

'Where are you going?' His face appeared round the corner.

'Didn't you see the notice? All first years are supposed to be in sick bay in ten minutes. Some talk from Dr Payne or something . . .'

Twenty-six

'What's Shona got, Dr Payne?'

'Is it catching?'

'Is it a rare disease?'

'Stop, stop!' Dr Payne held up her big hands and smiled round at everybody. 'That's exactly what I'm here to talk to you about.'

She pushed herself back so she was sitting on the desk. 'What's wrong with Shona,' she began, 'is that she hasn't enough vitamins and minerals and all the other things her body needs to keep her healthy and keep her dancing. And why not?' She paused for dramatic effect, opening her eyes really wide. 'I'll tell you why not! Because Shona has been dieting.'

There was silence. Sadie and I looked at one another.

'Now,' Dr Payne shifted herself on the desk a little. 'You might say diets aren't dangerous, are they? Lots of people go on diets. The TV's always advertising fantastic new ways to lose weight. Let me tell you,' Dr Payne's face became stern, she leant forward and held up a warning finger, 'dieting *is* dangerous, especially when you're still growing. You should never, ever do it unless a doctor tell you to.

'If you want to eat healthily, give up sweets and crisps by all means. But *replace* them with something.

130

Eat fruit and vegetables and bread and potatoes and meat—'

'Urgh!'

'Or cheese and nuts if you're vegetarian, Alex, OK?' Dr Payne nodded at him. 'To dance, you need strong muscles and bones. If you don't eat well, you might scupper your chances of ever being strong enough to be a dancer!'

Sadie put her hand up. 'Will Shona be OK?' she asked anxiously.

Dr Payne smiled. 'Yes, I'm glad to say she will. But she's gone home now for lots of rest. Her doctor at home will watch her very carefully. She won't be allowed back to school until she's definitely strong enough, and until she's eating properly.'

Dr Payne looked round, waiting to see if there were any more questions. No one put their hand up.

'OK, that's it folks – end of lecture. But if anyone's worried about this subject, do come and see me, and we can have a private chat about it.'

There was a buzz of chatter as everyone got to their feet.

'Oh, and Luci Simpson,' called Dr Payne above the noise. 'Can you stay behind for a minute?'

Dr Payne waited till the room had emptied, then turned to me with a smile. 'This particular cloud has a silver lining for you, doesn't it?'

I grinned sheepishly. 'I guess.'

'Well, I'm sure you'll do brilliantly.' She buried her hands in her trouser pockets. 'Look – before

Shona's parents picked her up earlier today, she gave me a message. Apparently her aunt had bought three tickets for tomorrow night's performance, and she won't be wanting them now. Shona thought you should have them – your family won't have had a chance to book tickets—'

'They don't even know, yet,' I said.

'I thought as much.' Dr Payne nodded. 'Shall I ask Miss Featherstone to call your mother?'

I hesitated. 'I don't suppose I could call, could I? I mean, just this once . . .'

'Since it's a bit of a special case,' said Dr Payne kindly, 'I'll see what I can do.'

Twenty-seven

It was ringing. I put my finger in my other ear and turned my back to Miss Featherstone.

'Hello?' said a familiar voice.

'Mum! It's me—'

'Luci? I thought you weren't allowed phone calls.'

'We're not. I'm ringing from Miss Featherstone's office—'

'Is it some emergency?'

'Sort of. A good one. Listen – you know this show I'm an understudy for? Well, someone's had to drop out – the main child's part – and I'm going on instead. Tomorrow night.'

There was a squeal from Mum and I had to hold the phone away from my ear. I think even Miss Featherstone could hear it.

'And there are three spare tickets, so you and Paul and Frankie can come!'

There was a pause.

'Hello?' I said. I could see Miss Featherstone looking at me over her spectacles, and I turned away from her again.

'Oh, Luci,' Mum sounded apologetic. 'I'm afraid it's Frankie's Christmas concert tomorrow night at school. Paul and I have promised her we'll go. She's playing a recorder solo.'

Her words sank in. I glanced at Miss Featherstone, who was pretending to read something, though she was obviously listening.

'But this is a real theatre,' I hissed into the phone. 'My first proper part . . .'

'You're doing more than one performance though, right?' Mum said brightly.

'Well, yes. But it's not the same.' I thought back to that letter from Pippa's mother. Now I knew how Pippa felt.

'I know it's not quite the same, honey, but we *have* promised Frankie, and she's only doing her concert once. We'll come to the very next performance we can get tickets for.'

My brain knew it was reasonable. They'd come to see me as soon as they could. They had Frankie to think about too, and she'd got in first.

I knew all this, but somehow I still felt that it was as if they didn't care. The first night was important – other people's parents had got there for the first night – even Ella's, all the way from Edinburgh, and even though they couldn't really afford the train fare.

'Yeah, fine,' I said. I knew I sounded sarcastic. Miss Featherstone was definitely giving me funny looks now.

'Luci,' I heard Mum's voice saying. 'Don't be like that.'

'Like what?' I said rudely. 'I told you it's fine. You just have a good time at Frankie's thing. I hope she plays in tune.'

I felt horrible as I said it, but I couldn't help myself.

Mum's voice sounded tired and worried. 'Sorry, honey,' she said. 'Oh jeepers. There's someone at the door. I've got to go. Look, I'll ring the theatre and get tickets first thing tomorrow. OK?'

'OK.'

'Bye now, honey. Love you.'

'Bye.' I put the phone down and, without looking at Miss Featherstone, I ran from the room.

Twenty-eight

'Cheer up, Luci – it's not the end of the world,' said Ella, rubbing the last of the greasy foundation into my cheeks. 'Look down now while I do your eyeshadow.'

'I know, I know. It's just—'

'This is your half-hour call, ladies and gentlemen. Half an hour please,' came the voice over the tannoy.

'Oh, help!' I tugged at Ella's dressing-gown. 'Do we have enough time?'

'Plenty,' laughed Ella. 'As long as you *look down*. And stop jigging your feet so much!'

I did as I was told and Ella got on with the eyeshadow.

'Now look up.'

'Just what?' said Sadie, glancing my way in the mirror, as she did her own make-up. 'What were you going to say?'

'It's just—' I found myself jigging my feet again, and stopped. 'What with half-term being so miserable, and this show meaning I'll miss out on loads of the Christmas fun at home, it somehow feels like – like Mum, Paul and Frankie are kind of settling down as a family without me.' I picked some fluff off my dressing-gown. 'I wanted them in the audience tonight just to prove . . . well, to prove they care about me being part of the family too.'

Ella looked shocked. 'Of *course* they do!'

'My parents didn't come to *my* first performance,' pointed out Pippa, getting up from her chair and reaching for her Act One costume.

Yeah, I thought, and from what I've heard, I don't like them an awful lot – but I just said, 'I guess so.'

'Right – you're done!' said Ella.

'Thanks.' I stood up and tapped my feet, going through the first scene in my mind.

Suddenly I was seized with the most awful panic. 'Jeepers! What on earth comes after the four skips and *échappé* into second?'

'Two claps and jump your feet together!' chorused Sadie, Ella and Pippa.

I grinned. 'Thanks, guys.'

'Overture and beginners. Overture and beginners, please,' the tannoy buzzed.

'Help, help, help!' I muttered under my breath, tucking the last wisp of hair into my cap.

'Just one more thing,' said Sadie, holding a large envelope towards me.

'Hurry up, girls!' called Mrs Pondswell from the dressing-room door.

'Open it – quick!' said Ella, as she and Pippa huddled round me.

I tore the envelope open. Inside was a big, homemade card. On the front was a drawing of me in the Tiny Tim costume, taking a bow on stage.

'It's brilliant!' I laughed.

Inside was the message: 'Break a leg Luci! Lots of love, Sadie, Ella and Pippa.' Then, in Pippa's handwriting, it said at the bottom: 'PS In case you didn't know, "break a leg" is what theatre people say for "good luck".'

I stood the card in front of my mirror, then turned and gave my three friends a hug.

'Do you intend to take part in the show this evening?' snapped Mrs Pondswell sarcastically. 'Because if you don't get a move on you'll have missed it!'

'Luci – you're doing great!' exclaimed Sadie, catching me as I raced up the stairs just before the interval. 'Are you enjoying it?'

I grinned over my shoulder. 'You bet! Did you hear the clapping after Scene Two? I reckon the audience loves it!'

'It's even better than the first night,' panted Sadie. 'Must be you that makes the difference!'

'Dead cert!' I laughed. 'Well – at least I haven't made any mistakes yet. Though I did tread on Jeremy's toe in the street scene, and he swore at me under his breath.'

'So much for dignified ballet dancers!'

Back in the dressing-room I had to change costumes again. I felt better now I'd got halfway through the performance, though the trickiest bit was still to come: at the end of Act Two, I had a solo, and I felt really nervous about it.

'You'll wear yourself out!' said Ella, as I went through the steps in the dressing-room for the umpteenth time.

'Second half beginners to the stage, please,' came the stage manager's voice.

This was it. I checked myself in front of the mirror, gave a last thumbs-up to Sadie, Ella and Pippa, and headed for the stairs.

My solo came in the bit of the story where Scrooge is shown the future by one of the Christmas ghosts. Scrooge sees that if he carries on being mean and horrible and not helping his worker, Bob, then Bob's little son Tiny Tim will die.

Robin had made up shaky little steps for Tiny Tim's solo, and I had to show the audience as I did them that I was very ill and sad. At the end I had to stagger and fall in a heap, with Scrooge and the Christmas ghost watching from the side of the stage.

As the music struck up, I took a deep breath, and stepped out from behind the scenery into the spotlight.

For a moment all I could think about was how empty the stage seemed, with just me dancing on it, and how big the theatre was, with its sea of dark faces out in front of me. But I remembered my steps and soon I was throwing myself into being Tiny Tim.

I don't know what made me look at the audience a few minutes later – really look, not just glance, which was all I'd done before. It was when I was down at the front of the stage, and I'd just done a skittering little *pas de chat,* when I turned my head, and something on the front row caught my eye.

It was a pair of stripy legs. Tights like Mum wears, I thought to myself, doing my spring points, and clutching my head in my hands as if I felt ill. Then I looked again, and my heart lurched.

It *was* Mum. And next to her sat Paul. Next to him sat Frankie.

I couldn't believe my eyes. I blinked and looked again – and they were still there. I was so gobsmacked that it was only after a moment or two I realised I'd stopped dancing.

Help! Where was I in the music now? In my confusion, I completely forgot what step came next – and I'd missed the beat for it anyway. I looked from side to side into the wings, but there was no one to help me. There was nothing else for it: I began to make up some steps.

I did a run and a little *jeté,* several *glissades* across the stage, and then mimed some coughing. Luckily I knew when the end of the music was coming, so at least I collapsed on the floor at the right time.

The audience broke into thunderous applause. But I hardly heard it. As soon as the lights blacked out, I ran into the wings.

Twenty-nine

My heart felt as if it had leapt into my throat. Tears were pricking at my eyes. I wiped them away roughly with the back of my sleeve.

I couldn't face going back to the dressing-room straight away, so I ran to the prop room Shona had dragged me into two days before. I didn't bother to put the light on – I just sat in the darkness and sobbed.

I'd messed up – and there was no chance the audience hadn't noticed. Robin would be furious.

Madame's words came back to me: 'If Mr Bell considers you are not dancing well enough, he will call upon David to take your place.'

I knew it – I'd blown the part. Thank goodness, I thought blearily, Mum, Paul and Frankie had seen the show tonight – because they wouldn't have got another chance after all.

From the music seeping into the little room, I soon realised that I had to come out, or I'd miss my next scene on stage. I licked my finger, and wiped underneath my eyes – I hoped that my eyeliner hadn't run too much. Then I stood up, smoothed down my costume, and went back into the wings.

'Once again!' boomed Marion, the stage manager.

The curtain flew up in front of us and the dancers stepped forward in their rows. The audience was a mass of smiling faces above clapping hands, and the applause just seemed to go on and on.

Taking our cue from Jeremy, who was in the middle of the front row, we all bowed together. People in boxes at the sides of the stage were throwing down carnations – and one landed right at my feet, a red one. I picked it up and waved it towards Mum and Paul. They grinned at me and clapped harder than ever. Mum put two fingers in her mouth and did a really loud whistle.

When the curtain came down for the last time, all I could think of was seeing them. I needed a great big hug.

'Where do you think you're going?' said a sharp voice behind me.

I could hardly get the words out quick enough. 'It's my mum and step-dad and sister. They're out there. Can I just go through and—' I pointed to the door that led from the backstage area into the auditorium.

Marion shook her head at me. 'Certainly not!' she said. 'No professional performer ever goes into the auditorium in make-up and costume. Go up to the dressing-room and get changed. Your family can wait for you at the stage door.'

I sighed impatiently, but Marion was too scary to argue with. Backtracking, I headed for the stairs and raced up to the dressing-room.

Five minutes later, my face still greasy with make-up remover, I was back downstairs again. There were plenty of people milling about, but none of them were Mum, Paul and Frankie.

Then I heard Henry's voice.

'Come on, now, ladies and gentlemen,' he was saying, 'They'll be out in a minute. Just keep back, will you?'

The stage door banged shut and he appeared in the hallway, smoothing his hair.

'My, they're a keen lot tonight,' he said, winking at me. 'There's a mad woman at the front who looks ready to flatten me.'

'She hasn't got red and black stripy tights on, by any chance?' I asked.

'Now . . .' Henry rubbed his chin. 'Come to think of it, she has.'

'That's my mum!' I cried. 'Please will you let her in? There'll be a man and a girl with her too. *Please!*'

Henry chuckled. 'Keep your hair on.' And he headed back to the stage door.

'Honey! You were great!' Mum enveloped me in a bear hug. I never wanted her to let go.

'My turn!' said Paul, picking me up and twirling me round.

'How come you're here?' I asked breathlessly.

'My school got flooded!' Frankie said, bouncing up and down in delight. 'The pipes burst – it was great!'

'So they cancelled the concert,' explained Mum.

'We had to race down here as fast as the old banger would go!' said Paul.

'Great show!' Mum grinned. 'I'm so proud of you!' She gave me another hug.

'I made some dreadful mistakes,' I said.

'Couldn't tell,' said Paul.

'Really?'

He nodded. 'Look – I'm afraid we can't stay long; the car's on a meter, and—' He looked at his watch. 'Damn! I'd better go and get it – it'll have a ticket by now.'

'You go,' Mum said to him. 'Pick me and Frankie up out at the front in a minute.'

'OK.' With a kiss for me, Paul left.

'This show should be in the West End,' Mum began, but then she spotted something and grabbed my arm. 'Luci! I know that face. It's – it's –'

I looked across, and saw that Pippa had come down too, and was standing in the corner with a woman who had the same pale hair and long nose. 'It's Clara Parnell, Mum,' I told her. 'Pippa's mother. She used to be a famous ballerina.'

'That's it!' Mum beamed delightedly. 'I saw her once on stage in Sydney. She was mind-blowing. Hey,' Mum plucked at my sleeve. 'Will you introduce me, honey? Will you?'

'Aw, Mum . . .'

'Go on, Luci. Be a sport.'

'OK.' I dragged Mum over to where Pippa and Mrs Parnell were standing, deep in conversation.

144

Well, Mrs Parnell was deep in saying something to Pippa. Pippa didn't seem to be saying much back.

'It wasn't too bad, darling, but you must use more *épaulement*,' I heard as we approached. Suddenly I felt a bit squeamish about butting in. But Mum was breathing over my shoulder like an excited pony, so I didn't have much choice.

'Hey, Pips,' I said, as casually as I could. Pippa turned, and for an instant I saw a look on her face I hadn't seen before – kind of vulnerable, like she was really young. But then I blinked, and the usual haughty Pippa was staring back at me again.

'Yes?' Pippa's mother had turned too, and had fixed her eyes on my mother, with such a look of astonishment I wanted to burst out giggling.

'I just wanted to introduce—' I began. 'Pippa, this is my mum, Janine. Mum, this is Pippa, and this is Pippa's mum—'

'Mrs Parnell-James,' said Pippa's mother loftily, tilting her chin up and her nose in the air just the same way Pippa did. Now I knew where she got it from!

She held out her hand, in its soft leather glove, for my mum to shake. Mum's pudgy fingers, with their bright red nails, closed round it and pumped it up and down enthusiastically.

'Delighted to meet you!' said Mum, grinning so widely her mouth looked in danger of bursting out of her face. 'An honour! A real honour!'

I looked at my mum and Pippa's mum. Mrs Parnell-

James was really elegant, wearing the sort of clothes that aren't flashy – but you just know they cost a bomb. She had little high-heeled court shoes on, that made it look as if her slender legs went on forever, and her hair was swept up gracefully into one of those pleats – French pleats I think you call them – at the back of her head. She looked like royalty.

My mum, on the other hand, was wearing blue lace-up boots and a bright yellow jumper dress. You couldn't have called her elegant, but she looked great. Her chunky red earrings and the red and blue spotty scarf in her hair were the perfect finishing touches. Pippa's mother was looking at her like she was something out of a zoo or a circus. Suddenly I felt so proud of my mum I wanted to hug her right then and there.

'Come on.' I nudged her, as she was still standing grinning at Mrs Parnell-James, who looked like she badly wished Mum would let go of her hand.

'Oh, right – well, bye-bye, now,' said Mum, and followed me back to where Frankie was using the battered sofa as a trampoline.

Behind us, I heard Pippa's mother say, 'Who on *earth* are those people, Pippa?' But I didn't hear what Pippa said in reply.

Thirty

Far too soon, Mum and Frankie had disappeared, swallowed up like Paul by the crowd still swarming outside the stage door. I was sad to say goodbye, but the thought of being home for Christmas in just a week and a half bucked me up. And I'd done quite enough crying for one night.

A minute later, I was clattering up to the dressing-room at full pelt. As I rounded one corner, taking the concrete steps two at a time, I cannoned straight into Robin, who was coming down.

'Hey, hey!' he laughed, catching hold of my arms to stop me from bowling him over completely. 'Not so fast!'

I gulped. The excitement of seeing Mum, Paul and Frankie had wiped the whole disaster of Act Two out of my mind. Now it came flooding back. I shifted from foot to foot, hoping Robin wouldn't want to talk to me about it just yet.

'Act Two,' he said.

Uh-oh.

'It looked a little different from how I'd imagined it.'

I nodded and stared at the handrail on the wall next to me. 'Sorry,' I mumbled. 'I – I got mixed up and forgot the steps.'

'I thought as much,' said Robin, folding his arms. 'Can you remember what you did?'

I nodded. It made me wince just thinking about it.

'Good,' said Robin. 'Because I want you to do the same next time. And teach it to the Team B Tiny Tim, will you? I like it better than the steps I made up.'

I looked at him. 'Really?'

He laughed. 'Really,' he said. 'I never thought that scene looked quite right anyhow. You had a flash of inspiration, obviously!' He laughed again. 'Fancy being a choreographer one day?'

'You bet!' I said.

Robin put a hand on my shoulder. 'Well, don't do it too soon,' he said. 'Or I might be out of a job.'

I laughed.

'And well done for the rest of the show too,' he added. 'You were great!'

Just then I heard footsteps behind me. I turned in time to see Miss Latimer rounding the corner. My stomach lurched. I hadn't even known she was coming tonight.

'Ah, Daphne!' said Robin, as she looked up and seemed just as startled to see us. 'I was just talking to your star pupil here. Didn't she do well? You must be really proud of her!'

'Er, yes.' Miss Latimer looked at me awkwardly. She bent down and kissed the air near my cheek. 'Well done, my dear.'

'She's a credit to your teaching, Daphne!' said Robin, with a mischievous twinkle in his eye.

Miss Latimer smiled at him in some confusion and, making her excuses, hurried back down the stairs the way she had come.

'Robin!' I'd just remembered something. 'Miss Latimer said she was going to tell you not to give me that part.'

Robin nodded. 'That's right. She did.'

'Then . . .' My voice tailed off, and I frowned in bewilderment.

'*Then* I got a phone call,' said Robin. 'Someone told me that on the opening night, Shona fainted before the last scene and you went on instead of her. So I knew just how brilliant you were! And I've guessed why you might not see eye to eye with Miss Latimer . . .' It was Robin's turn now to let his voice tail off. He came past me down the stairs, and checked round the corner, as if he was expecting Miss Latimer to be there, listening.

'Someone phoned you? Who?' I gasped.

Robin looked back up to me and raised his eyebrows. Then he smiled as footsteps clattered on the stairs above and a figure appeared.

'Oh, here she comes now!' he said. 'Look – I've got to go.' And, with a laugh, he disappeared.

'You? You rang Robin?'

Sadie stood on the step above me, grinning. 'Might have done.'

I thought back. 'When did you get the chance?

Ah! *That's* why you were late for English!'

'Well,' Sadie shrugged. 'I had to make up for the audition somehow, didn't I? Giving you all that bad advice that meant you didn't get a part.'

'Sadie, thanks so much—' I began, but she cut me off.

'Look – are you coming up to the dressing-room or what?' she said, wagging a finger at me and grinning. 'Mrs Pondswell says if you're not back there in two seconds she'll give you four black marks.'

I laughed. 'That sounds like her!

'But right now,' I added, as Sadie headed back up the stairs and I raced after her, 'if she gave me a *million*, I couldn't care less!'

If you've enjoyed this book,
look out for the other *Ballerina* stories

Sadie's Ballet School Dream

She's the best ballerina there is.
Talented, beautiful and famous throughout the world.
In her dreams, that is.
Sadie hasn't even started ballet lessons!
Then before she knows it she's invited to audition for the Evanova School – it's a chance for her dream to come true.

Pippa on Pointe

Pointe shoes at last!
It's what all the friends had been waiting for.
Except Pippa.
She's got a secret – and it's about to come out!
How can she hide the truth from her best friends?

Ella's Last Dance

Gentle, talented Ella is chosen to perform a solo in the school concert to celebrate Madame's eightieth birthday – and she's top of the class at school work. But then disaster strikes – Ella will have to give up her dancing career – her parents can no longer afford the fees.

There is a scholarship, but will Ella win it?

Someone is out to destroy her chances.

Can she find out who it is before it's too late?

Ballerinas
Harriet Castor

☐	65129 6	Sadie's Ballet School Dream	£3.50
☐	65130 X	Luci in the Spotlight	£3.50
☐	65131 8	Pippa on Pointe	£3.50
☐	65132 6	Ella's Last Dance	£3.50

All Hodder Children's books are available at your local bookshop or newsagent, or can be ordered direct from the publisher. Just tick the titles you want and fill in the form below. Prices and availability subject to change without notice.

Hodder Children's Books, Cash Sales Department, Bookpoint, 39 Milton Park, Abingdon, OXON, OX14 4TD, UK. If you have a credit card you may order by telephone – (01235) 831700.

Please enclose a cheque or postal order made payable to Bookpoint Ltd to the value of the cover price and allow the following for postage and packing:
UK & BFPO – £1.00 for the first book, 50p for the second book, and 30p for each additional book ordered up to a maximum charge of £3.00.
OVERSEAS & EIRE – £2.00 for the first book, £1.00 for the second book, and 50p for each additional book.

Name ....

Address ....

....

....

If you would prefer to pay by credit card, please complete:
Please debit my Visa/Access/Diner's Card/American Express (delete as applicable) card no:

Signature ....

Expiry Date ....